I0691610

The Torn Slipper

by

Kimberlee R. Mendoza

This is a work of fiction. Names, characters, places, and incidents are either the product of the author's imagination or are used fictitiously, and any resemblance to actual persons living or dead, business establishments, events, or locales, is entirely coincidental.

The Torn Slipper

COPYRIGHT © 2022 by Kimberlee Ruth Mendoza

All rights reserved. No part of this book may be used or reproduced in any manner whatsoever without written permission of the author or The Wild Rose Press, Inc. except in the case of brief quotations embodied in critical articles or reviews.
Contact Information: info@thewildrosepress.com

Cover Art by *Kim Mendoza*

The Wild Rose Press, Inc.
PO Box 708
Adams Basin, NY 14410-0708
Visit us at www.thewildrosepress.com

Publishing History
First Edition, 2022
Trade Paperback ISBN 978-1-5092-4738-7
Digital ISBN 978-1-5092-4739-4

Published in the United States of America

Dedication

To Kali at Lindenwood University and the faculty at Wayland Baptist University for their continued encouragement.

Chapter One

A Little Over 2 Years Ago

Snide whispers. Pursed lips. Gazes traversed my body like I had thousands of bugs on me—what was the deal with these girls? I drew my notebook closer under my chin and hurried faster down the crowded high school hallway toward my next class. I sensed each scowl and detected every nasty word about me. When I reached Room 203, I exhaled with relief. Well, for like 2.3 seconds, when a couple of girls stopped talking in order to shoot darts of disgust my way. You know the kind? Glares with flared nostrils and lips that swelled into duck face, as if I just stepped into a heap of week-old garbage.

I faced away and crossed to my spot. *What did I do?* I thumbed through the memories in my brain. Nothing came forward to admit my crime. I peeked over at them again, but sorry I did. *Ignore them. Maybe if I can't see them, they can't see me.* I slid onto my lab stool and stared front.

"Oh my gosh, Cindy!" Gabby squealed.

The sound reverberated from the door all the way to my table.

She smacked the countertop hard, then slid around to sit on the stool. "You are like the most hated girl in the entire school!"

1

You don't have to sound so happy about it. "Yeah, I kind of got that." I leaned forward and narrowed my eyes at the annoying redhead. "Why?"

Her twin Charlotte spun around on the stool in the row in front of us and giggled. The two girls weren't identical, but both were awkward in their own way. Gabby had grown tall and gangly; Charlotte stopped at short and stumpy. Both had frizzy red hair, freckles, braces, and occasional acne. Puberty had not been kind to either girl. Charlotte might be considered a tad more attractive than her sister, but not by much. Most people treated them like pariah, but I tried to be nice.

Pariah. I frowned. *Kind of like how I feel in this moment.* "What do you know?" I demanded again.

"Well…" Gabby licked her braces and leaned closer.

"It seems that…" Charlotte smiled and giggled again. Both girls exchanged looks, then tittered like birds in unison.

They could be so infuriating. I sucked in a deep breath to keep from screaming, reminding myself to be patient. I opened my mouth to say, "Get on with it," when Andy Scott walked in. Or should I say, strutted in. The baseball star exuded confidence. Tall, with dark, shoulder-length hair that fell over one eye. Sometimes he would flip it back and all the girls would swoon. In truth, all the girls—myself included—wanted him to be their boyfriend. Last month, Mr. Boyd had assigned him as my lab partner. I would forever be grateful to Mr. Boyd, no matter how boring his lectures were.

"Hey," Andy said to me, before eyeing Gabby who sat in his seat.

A red hue, brighter than her hair, blanketed her

face. She emitted an embarrassed cackle and stumbled off his seat to her stool in front by Charlotte.

"Hey, yourself," I said, despite being slightly distracted by the two sisters whispering in front of me.

"I wanted to ask you something."

I pulled my stare from them and gazed into his beautiful hazel eyes. Well, the one I could see.

"You know how the homecoming dance is in a few weeks?"

I swallowed. My heart thumped in my throat. "Yeah?"

"Want to go with me?"

My stare stayed on the cute guy probably a moment too long, but when I glanced up, I saw all the girls in the class foaming at the mouth. *Awe, now the loathing makes more sense.* "Yeah, totally." I hoped I said that nonchalantly, because internally I danced the Cabbage Patch around the room.

"Cool." He winked, then reached for a beaker at the end of the counter.

I remembered little else. We made some formula in our workbook. I don't remember. Mr. Boyd talked. Not sure what he said. Hopefully, nothing on the test, because the only chemistry I cared about had to do with Andy and his close proximity.

****

"Well, you're sure smiling." Mom placed a tray of fruit on the long dining room table, before tucking a strand of her shoulder-length blonde hair out of her face.

"You're not going to believe it. I mean, I can't, and it happened to me. It's super exciting news." I slid into the fancy antique chair and flapped a cloth napkin into my lap, still smiling.

Dad entered, kissed Mom's cheek, then sat across the table.

Even though the table stretched the entire room, we all hunkered down at the end.

"I love exciting news. Do tell."

"Andy Scott asked me to homecoming."

My parents exchanged glances.

Dad lifted his dark groomed eyebrows as he met my gaze. "Andy Scott? What kind of boy is Andy Scott?"

"Only the best kind of boy, Dad. Every girl at school wants him, but he asked me." I giggled again. "Me!"

Mom patted my hand. "Well, of course, he did. He obviously has great taste."

"And all the girls hate me now."

My parents frowned and eyed each other again.

They always did that. Some kind of secret language. Super annoying.

"I'm sure that's not true." Mom frowned.

I reached for another grape and shrugged. "I don't care. It's not like I get along with most of them anyway."

Mom's frown deepened. "I didn't know you were having trouble making friends."

"It's okay. I don't care." That might have been a lie. Of course, I *wanted* friends. Who didn't? But I never said the right thing at the right time. Sometimes I acted shy or made an awkward comment. But who cared? Andy Scott saw something in me, and that was worth 10,000 friends.

Dad glopped a spoonful of red potatoes onto his

plate. "Do we need to talk about that?"

"No, seriously, I'm fine. I've got friends who matter. I'm cool. Really."

He stared at me for a moment longer, then returned to serving himself more food.

The head cook and housekeeper, Rosa, peeked in the doorway. "I'm heading out tonight. Do you need anything else, Mr. Tremaine?"

"No, everything looks great. Thanks, Rosa."

Her plump cheeks turned up in a grin, and she nodded. "Night."

"Night," we said in unison.

Mom grinned. "So, now we need to go shopping and buy you a dress worthy of Andy…"

"Scott." I beamed. "Really?"

"Of course. You can't go to a formal without the perfect dress. We can go tomorrow afternoon, if you're free."

I leapt out of my chair with a shriek and hugged her neck. "Thanks, Mom."

Chapter Two

One Month, Three Weeks, and Two Days Later

The night of homecoming, I stood in the mirror, admiring my new dress. The black heart bodice shaped my developing figure perfectly. I especially liked the charcoal tulle with a few diamond sparkles that sprinkled both the top overlay and the skirt. I couldn't believe it.

My first dance, and I had a date. Not any date— Andy Scott! My stomach skipped. I rubbed a hand over my bodice and giggled.

Mom's reflection filled the mirror. "You look so pretty."

I spun and grinned. "You think he'll like it?"

"Unless he's blind, he'd better." She winked.

I faced the mirror again, swaying side to side, watching the material shift with my moves. I liked the sound it made. I bobbed back and forth, to hear it again and again. *Swish, swish, swish.*

"What time does he get here?" she asked.

I glanced at my phone. "In a half-hour, I think."

"Did you eat dinner?" she asked

"Just a snack. There's supposed to be food at the dance. Not that I'm hungry at all." I hadn't been able to eat anything all day.

"Yeah, boys have a way of doing that. When we

6

like them, we can't eat a thing. When we break up, we can't stop eating." She laughed, then touched my shoulder. "I got you something."

"Really?" I faced her again, bouncing on my tiptoes. "What?"

"Here." She handed me a sky-blue gift bag the size of my palm.

I undid the gold ribbon at the top and withdrew a tiny silver box. I glanced up.

She nodded toward it.

I lifted the lid and gasped. An onyx teardrop charm surrounded by a few diamonds rested on a bed of white satin. It matched my dress perfectly. I squealed. "Oh, Mom. I love it."

"I'm so glad." She winced and grabbed the side of her head.

"Mom?" My smile faltered. "Are you okay?"

Her mouth turned up in a pained grin. "Yeah, sorry. I've had a slight headache all day. It's nothing. I just need to take something, and I'll be fine." She reached for the necklace with one hand and twirled her finger in a circle with the other. "Turn around. I'll put it on you."

I spun back, making sure the dress swished once more as I glanced in the mirror.

Mom lifted the chain over my head and clasped it at my neck. "There. Perfect. What do you think?"

I fingered the black stone in the reflection in front of me. The diamonds glimmered in the overhead light. "It's perfect. Thanks—"

Something thudded behind me. I checked over my shoulder, but Mom no longer stood there. Rather I found her crumpled on the floor, eyes closed and face ashen. "Mom!" I screamed. "Mom!" My heart pounded in my chest, and my stomach soured. I ran to the doorway. "Dad!" When he didn't come right away, I yelled louder, "Dad! It's Mom! Dad!"

Dad poked his head at the bottom of the stairs. "What's wrong?"

"It's Mom," I repeated. "Something's wrong with Mom."

He sprinted up the stairs, two at a time.

When he reached the room, I stepped back to let him enter. His gaze fell to his wife, and his eyes enlarged. He folded to her side and touched two fingers to her neck.

"Is she okay? What's wrong with her?" I knelt on her other side, sobbing.

He didn't answer; instead, he withdrew his cell phone from his jacket pocket. His fingers shook against the screen. "Shoot!" He opened and closed his fist, then tried three times to dial 9-1-1 before it successfully went through. It rang twice.

"9-1-1, what's your emergency?" the operator said through the speaker.

"My wife...something is wrong..." He tapped the icon and brought the phone to his ear. "She has fallen...she...she's not breathing." He paused for their response. "No, she's been fine." He paused. "Not that I know of."

"She had a headache," I whispered.

"What's that, Sweetheart?" he asked me, then dipped his head. "No sorry, my daughter said something. One second. What did you say?"

"She said she had a headache all day." I tucked a strand of her hair away from her face and sniffed.

8

"She had a headache all day?"

I nodded.

He repeated it to the operator.

I heard little else. I stroked her hand. It felt icy and hollow. I prayed—waiting, wondering—scared.

The EMTs arrived and thrust me aside.

A worker tugged a cup with a bag over her mouth, and another guy stuck a needle in her arm.

Feeling numb, I crawled onto my bed, hugged my pillow, and watched wide-eyed as they placed her onto a gurney.

The EMTs scrambled to get her loaded, but then stopped. A loud electronic screech filled the air, then they hit her with two metal paddles. Her chest catapulted up, then fell back hard. They did it again, twice more. The third EMT continued to press on her chest.

I couldn't watch any more. My body shivered. I pulled a blanket over me, but it didn't help. The cold settled deep in my bones with no relief. I heard them roll her out, but I didn't watch. I closed my eyes instead and sobbed deep into my pillow.

At some point, Dad appeared at my side, helped me stand, and guided me out the door.

The maid said something about Andy as we passed her in the hall.

But I didn't care. I ignored her, dazed, and trudged toward the limo in front of the house.

We rode to the hospital to only the sound of my muffled cries. My eyes, now swollen and burning, made the world in front of me blurry and indistinguishable. My chest ached from quick, panicked breaths. My head pounded deep inside my skull.

Dad combed my hair with his fingers and spoke words like, "it will be all right," and "don't worry about it honey" or "Mom's strong" or "Have faith." But those expressions did little to make me feel better. We both knew they were lies anyway. Especially when the doctor revealed the cause of her collapse.

A man in a white coat approached us and said a few things, followed up by, "I'm sorry." Empty words, filled with pain. The doctor went on to explain that a brain aneurism had killed her. No time to say goodbye. Just dead... In a mere second... Without warning... Gone.

I have no recollection of how I got home that night. Someone, maybe the limo driver, or my aunt, or was it the maid? I don't remember, but someone tucked me into bed early in the morning. The mysterious person didn't undress me. Or perhaps I wouldn't allow them to. Who knew? I only remembered I slept in my dream dress that night. The dress never made it to the dance, but I wore it to my mother's funeral. Though it was black, my aunt deemed it inappropriate—something about the sequins and tulle not being serious enough, but it was the last thing my mom and I did together. In my mind, the dress could not be more appropriate. Enough so, I wore it for over a week before my dad made me change. I hated when I took it off. Removing the dress felt final. But after that day, I never wore it again.

Chapter Three

Andy tried to talk to me, but I ignored him. Nothing personal as I ignored everyone. Though I traversed the school halls, I felt ghostly—out of body. I had no desire to be friends with anyone or to talk to another soul. They could not appreciate my pain. No one would understand. Deeper and deeper, I fell into a pit of desolation. Every day, I had my own personal pity party—a regular rager—and no one else was invited.

Dad tried to reach me. Occasionally, I would let him in a tiny crack. He tried to make me smile with a joke or kind gesture, but any sort of happiness made me feel guilty. So, I didn't allow myself to experience any joy. I chopped off and dyed my hair platinum-blonde, got a tattoo on my wrist that read the date Mom died, and slept a lot.

This depression lingered months, okay to be honest, a few years, but eventually with the help of a therapist, I began to feel hope again. After graduation, I started to change for the better, until on the fateful day when Dad invited me to what he called a "special dinner."

I arrived at the hostess stand of the Blue de Bunia, a swanky restaurant on the water in Malibu, and glanced over the sea of people. My father waited in the far corner with an ocean view. I smiled and walked

11

toward him, then the room seemed to slow, and I stopped short.

A woman sat nestled against him, laughing, touching his arm, and whispering in his ear.

My lips pressed hard, and my eyes narrowed as I studied her. The intrusive, curly red-haired stranger appeared out of place in this high-class restaurant. She wore an embroidered peasant blouse, a stack of leather bracelets, and a thin, olive-green scarf wrapped like a headband around her head. A bohemian, hippie. Hardly high-class. Clearly, not someone who belonged here in this place.

She leaned into Dad's ear and whispered something.

He laughed loud like she had said the funniest thing he had ever heard.

My eyes narrowed. He did not tell me we would have company at this "special dinner," and I absolutely did not appreciate it. I could have run away, but curiosity held stronger than my fear, so I inched forward. The closer I got; I knew I recognized her. Not sure why or from where, but I had seen this woman before. Watching her hand touch his bicep again, my skin crawled. I stared at them, still a few tables away, wondering, *Could I do this?* I swayed on the balls of my feet forward, then backward. *Yes. I have to.*

Shaking off the fear and replacing it with anger, I prepared for war. I rolled my shoulders back, lifted my chin a little higher, took a deep breath, and weaved around the last few tables to join them. "Dad?"

His gaze shifted from the stranger's to mine. As it registered that I stood there, he rose, smiled, and gave me a hug and kiss on the cheek. "Hello, Sweetheart.

I'm glad you made it."

The woman placed a sesame breadstick on a small plate and also smiled.

I slid onto the velvet cushion and eyed her. "I thought we were eating *alone*."

"I wanted to surprise you." He smiled, then placed a hand on the bohemian's shoulder. "This is Meredith. And Meredith, this is my lovely daughter, Cynthia."

"It's very nice to finally meet you." She smiled a huge grin that cut through freckles and revealed a few crow's feet.

My "claws" extended in my thoughts. *Sure, natural beauty is great and all, but would it hurt to use a little makeup?* I acted as if the introduction had not occurred. "Are we going to order?"

"Cynthia, don't be rude."

Meredith continued to grin. "I've heard so much about you, and—"

"Funny, I haven't heard a thing about you," I said.

"Cynthia, I'm warning you." Dad leaned forward.

I knew not to push too much further. He had a threshold. I had towed the line for over a year now, but crossing it would be dangerous. Most likely, threatening to take away my allowance for starters. Something I could not part with, not with how I liked to live.

I shifted my stare back to him. He looked handsome in a designer navy blue suit and matching striped tie. As always, his gray speckled hair lay slicked to perfection, but his soothing smile had been replaced by an angry scowl. "I was only stating the truth, Dad. I promise, I wasn't trying to be rude." I closed the menu and folded my elbows over it on the table. "You look familiar, Meredith. Do I know you from somewhere?"

She grinned again. A black speck, probably a sesame seed, lay between her two middle teeth.

It gave me pleasure somehow.

"Yes, I am a waitress at Third Stop Café on Second and North. Your dad always sits in my section."

The two of them shared a knowing glance, followed by a lovesick giggle that about made me gag. Dad could not possibly have slummed this low. I glanced around, wishing I could share my thoughts out loud. I opened my mouth, ready to respond.

A server stepped to the table. "May I take your order?"

"I'm not hungry." I handed back the menu. I knew where this conversation would end—with me throwing a child's tantrum and storming out in a dramatic fashion. I prepared myself for that, playing and replaying the moment in my mind. Nothing my father said right now would change the appointed outcome. Rage fueled me, as heat traveled up my spine and into my neck and face. The way I saw it, the woman on my father's arm rested in my mother's chair. One that had only been vacated a few years ago. *How dare he.*

"Are you sure you don't want to eat?" Dad eyed me, his eyes soft with concern.

I answered with a nod.

He looked at the server. "I'll have the surf and turf. Medium rare, with loaded mashed potatoes, extra bacon, and a side of broccoli, and the woman next to me will have the vegetable platter."

"With a side of ranch, please," Meredith added.

"Did you want to add a salad or soup to your meals?" the server asked.

14

Dad glanced at Meredith, who shook her head. "No, I think we're good. Thank you."

"Very well." The server took both menus and left us to our uncomfortable situation.

"So, why are you here, Meredith?" I asked.

She glanced at my father with raised eyebrows.

He cleared his throat and rubbed his hands together.

For a moment, it seemed like he had choked on his words. "Meredith and I have been dating for six months," he said finally.

Despite having no appetite, I reached for a breadstick and snapped it. So many feelings threatened to overtake me—confusion, denial, anger, sadness, rage, sorrow. I had no idea how to respond, so I didn't. I waited, flicking sesame seeds off onto the white tablecloth.

"We didn't want to say anything until we were sure…"

My stomach churned. *Please don't say it. Please don't say it.* An unseen force locked my stare onto the table, unable to look at Dad. As if seeing him would make it happen. Everything in me begged, *please do not let my greatest fear become a reality. Please don't say it. I beseech you. Please don't say it.* Stars whirled in my vision; my head spun. Dizzy, I blinked to keep from blacking out. *Please don't say it.* Panic seized every nerve in my body. *Please…don't…say…it.*

"Cindy…" he said.

Slowly, I lifted my gaze to meet his.

The two regarded me, then each other, and then in unison, they both looked back at me. My father visibly swallowed, his Adam's apple bobbing up and down.

"We have decided to get married."

And with those six words, hell crash-landed in Southern California. Fire coursed through my bloodstream and threatened to seize my vision, as well. With nothing left to say, I dropped the mangled breadstick on the table, slid back in the chair, tossed the cloth napkin on the chair next to mine, raised on wobbly legs, and staggered like a drunk out of the restaurant as fast as I could. I faintly heard Dad behind me, but I ignored him. I chose to block out the rest. Or maybe I just could not remember.

Maybe, because that night marked my downward spiral into hades. The first night, I got wasted. The first night, I did not come home when I was supposed to. It had to be the last time I care about myself or anyone else and when I began a full withdrawal from the few friends I had and Dad. The inauguration of my being nasty to everyone I encountered. It birthed an "activation of a newfound attitude"—so Dad said.

In that moment, I did not care to be "the good daughter" any longer. I had been that, and what did it get me? A dead mother and stepmonster. Sure, Meredith appeared nice. But she didn't *belong* in my life. In *our* life. Not sleeping in my parent's bed. Not cooking in my mother's kitchen. Not stealing my father's heart. I despised her, not for who she was, but for what she took.

Chapter Four

Present Day

"Useless!" I flung my cell phone onto the satin comforter and retrieved a gold bell from the end table by my bed. "Where are you, good-for-nothing maid?"

The sound of tires cracked on the brick driveway outside the second-story window of our Wilshire home in Beverly Hills. I bounced off the four-poster bed and tucked back the drapes to peer below. Our limo looped the circular driveway and stopped just shy of the marble steps.

A chauffeur, dressed in the usual black suit and cap, stepped out of the driver's seat and strode around to the back door.

A new driver. I smashed my face against the window to get a better look. The guy had shaved dark hair, high cheekbones, and cappuccino skin—total eye candy. Of course, I could never go for him. *Puh-lease.* His profession made him totally undesirable. Blue collar, white collar—who cared. Workingmen were gross—sweaty, stinky, callused hands, dirty fingernails, and low pay. I grimaced. Besides, his paycheck couldn't buy one of my pant legs. I laughed and let the curtain flutter closed. "Eustace!" I rang the bell again.

The mousy waif appeared in the doorway, breathless and unkempt.

17

I scanned her from head to toe. The girl needed a serious makeover—caterpillars for eyebrows, no makeup, and stringy dishwater blonde hair, and so thin, her gray uniform swallowed her figure whole. How did one go out in the morning looking like that? Not that her appearance mattered. What civilized man would want to love a maid anyway? "Eustace, where were you? I had to ring twice."

"It's Eunice, ma'am."

"Potato, putah-toe. Whatever. Just answer my question. Where were you?"

"Sorry, I was helping Meredith with her pr—"

"Stop." I pinched my fingers together to indicate her silence. "Like I care what you were *going* to do. I'm more interested in what you *should* be doing right now. And that's bringing me a hot orange tea with a teaspoon of brown sugar and non-dairy creamer. Non-dairy. Don't be slipping me extra calories and lactose again. Understand?"

The maid stared without comment.

"And I'll take it on the balcony. Can you handle that? Or will I have to wait another hour and get a sprained wrist from all the ringing?"

"Yes, miss."

The waif shuffled toward me, instead of walking away like I wanted her to.

"Your sisters asked me to ask you—"

"Step, Useless. *Step*sisters." How I loathed those two morons. They tried to be sickly-sweet to me, but I saw through their diabolical plan. They sought to take my position in this home, but that would never happen. Not on my watch. Not while my heart still pumped. No nerdy girls would get to be the queen of my father's heart and home. That will forever be my role—to be head princess. "Remember, Useless, I come before Meredith. Me, always, me first. Got that?"

I strode to the walk-in closet and flung the double doors open at the same time. I loved being dramatic. A sense of power came with it. Something I learned years ago, it helped me get my way ninety-nine percent of the time, and the one percent people paid for it dearly.

The maid inched forward, still not leaving.

"What?" I snapped.

"Meredith has been good to you, like a mother, and—"

Heat rose in my chest and into my face. How dare she put those words in the same sentence. I flipped toward her with clenched fists and eyes narrowed. *"Like.* Key word, *like.* She is *not* my mother. Never will be. Ever. Do not ever confuse the two. You got that?"

The timid girl cowered back, hands in the air, shaking.

I'd admit, I felt a little bad. I didn't mean to frighten the poor girl. "Calm down, I'm not going to hurt you." I returned to the closet and glanced over my shoulder. "Just don't ever put Meredith and mother in the same context, you got me?"

The girl nodded. "I'm sorry, but your stepsisters came by for—"

"Are you still here?" I tossed a cardigan near her feet and shifted the hangers over, yawning as if bored. "And change your name. Eugene is an ugly name for a girl."

"It's Eunice."

"Still ugly. How about Anastasia or Brianna? Beautiful names. Yes, I like both. Which would you prefer?"

"I'll get your tea." The maid sniffed and hurried from the room.

I yanked a soft pink silk blouse from its perch and held it to my torso in the mirror.

"You should be nicer to her, Cynthia," Dad's voice boomed outside my closet.

I dropped the shirt and threw my arms around his neck. His designer gray suit smelled of spicy cologne. Dad was clean shaven and handsome—though in his early fifties, his high cheekbones and lack of wrinkles could put him at late thirties—easily. Of course, his six-foot-four stature made him not only attractive to the masses, but it also gave him presence. People feared and respected this man. I fingered his tie, tilting it into its rightful place. It always lay crooked, and I imagined he did that on purpose. He knew I would fix it. I always did. I smiled. "When did you get back?"

"An hour ago."

"You aren't leaving again?"

His mouth turned downward. "Unfortunately, yes."

I frowned. "Do you have a date with some gorgeous, hot blonde?"

His face tensed as he unwrapped from my arms and stepped back. "You know it is not a date."

Of course, I knew. I also realized I had hurt his feelings. I couldn't help myself. Feelings of bitterness still lingered thick in my heart between us. He had no right to marry so soon after my mother's death. Though I rarely voiced it, I harbored serious animosity. But per usual, I didn't say what I really felt. "Sorry, Dad. I just wondered. That's all."

"Nice try. I get what you're trying to do," he said.

"When are you going to accept Meredith as my new wife? It's been almost a year now."

I sensed his disappointment. But I didn't have it in me to give him a pass. "Do I have to put a time limit on it?"

"Cindy," he warned.

I pouted. "Fine. Go to your meeting then."

"Actually, travel. I'm flying to meet an investor for my next movie."

I deepened my pout. I hated being stuck in this house with *them*. The three women who did not belong here. "Please don't go. You just got back."

"You know I have to. And while I am away, please be nicer to the help."

"Why? They're being paid to do their job." I winked.

His mouth turned into a hard scowl. "Cynthia."

I giggled. His reaction always made it funnier to act like a brat. "So, where are you off to this time?"

"New York. Now give your old man a hug, so I can catch my plane on time." He held his arms out.

I crossed my arms. "And, if I don't hug you, will you stay?"

"Cynthia…"

"Okay. Fine." I filled them, tight and secure in that hold.

After a moment, he patted my back, an indication that he wanted me to let go. I always held on just a second more, but finally let go. Unhappy. Now he would leave.

He directed my chin with a crooked finger to face him. "Promise me, you'll be good."

"Me?" I blew a raspberry and batted at the air. "Of

course. Like always."

His mouth hardened. "I'm serious."

"I know."

He sighed, kissed the top of my head, then turned and started down the hall. "I'll see you at the end of the week."

I trailed behind him. "End of the week? You aren't serious?" My heart sunk even lower. In this entire world, I only cared about one thing—my dad. Without him around, I would be even more miserable than usual. "But our birthday party is on Friday." Though our birthdays were only a day apart, we always celebrated together.

"I'll be back in time for the party. Don't you worry." He stopped at the bottom stair and faced me with his warm smile.

The closed mouth grin that told me everything would be okay. His look had held me in the darkest of times. When monsters invaded my room in the middle of the night, his smile held me. When mean girls at school taunted me, it helped me through. When mom died, his smile was all I had to make me feel better. "Promise?" I asked, like a small child.

"I promise." He walked below my step, kissed my cheek, and, for a moment, stared with a reflective gaze. "You look so much like your mother did at this age."

A pool of tears invaded my eyes. I blinked them away. "So, what does the man who has everything want for his birthday this year?"

He sighed. "The truth?"

I nodded.

"For my daughter to start acting like an adult for once," he said.

I rolled my eyes. Same old, same old. *As if.* "What does that even mean, Dad?"

"Do you really need me to spell it out?" When I didn't answer, he responded, "You order the servants around, eat my food, spend my money, and whenever you leave, it's for some ridiculous party."

"I know, great life, huh?"

His eyes narrowed.

I wanted to laugh, but I didn't dare. "I don't understand the problem. Seriously, what's wrong with any of that?"

"See there, that *is* the problem. You have no concept of why that is wrong. You have no appreciation for anything. I put up with it for a while because I felt sorry for you, but you are no longer a kid, Cynthia. You're almost twenty-one." He took a deep, visible breath. "It's time."

"Time?" I put my hands in the air and shrugged. "For what?"

"To get a job."

A loud laugh thrust from my mouth before I could stop it. I covered my lips, amused more than ashamed. But then, his stern expression gave me pause. "Sorry, it's just, what do I need a job for? When I've got all this." I held out my arms, as if to encompass all of the wealth surrounding us—the tall arched windows, grandiose chandeliers, exotic Persian rugs, and million-dollar paintings. "Isn't that the point of a job? To get stuff."

"It's *my* stuff."

"Hardly."

"Keep it up, Cynthia, and you won't—" He checked his watch. "Oh, shoot. I've got to go. I'll call when I arrive, and we can continue this conversation then."

"Can't wait," I said dryly.

He rushed back down the steps and out the door.

I trudged to my room, hoping he had only been kidding. Get a job? *The man must be getting old and delusional.* I sat on the edge of my bed, feeling on edge. My striped tabby cat Skittles leapt on the mattress and slinked next to my thigh, rubbing her head on my leg. I scratched under her chin, and a purr followed. Her presence often soothed me. I needed that now. In the pit of my stomach, I knew my attitude upset Dad. But I couldn't help it. Right now, as much as I loved him, I didn't like him. In truth, he hurt me, too. Maybe more so, when he married *her.*

"Hello, Sweetheart."

Speak of the devil. As if on cue, to aid in my misery, my stepmonster Meredith appeared in the doorway with her normally annoying cheery disposition. "Now that your dad is gone, I need your help."

I didn't want to help this woman do anything. I studied her for a moment, without responding.

Her long red hair was swept up on the sides with tortoise shell combs to hold it in place. Her makeup done natural, as always, with a light gloss on her perfectly shaped lips and just enough powder to soften her freckles. Her loose, boho, white shirt and red gypsy skirt did little to cover her bodacious curves. No mystery why Dad married Meredith—thirty-six, twenty-four, thirty-six came to mind. But why did Meredith marry him? Easy—dollar signs. A waitress in Glendale, come on, could she be more of a cliché?

Probably the biggest reason why I resented her so much. That, and no one could replace my mother or should share Dad's heart. The thought of her moving in on either of those positions made her enemy number one.

Ignoring her, I dropped Skittles to the floor, then bent down and peered under my bed. "Where did I put my cell phone?" Though I pretended to look for my phone, I knew full well it sat a few feet away, plugged into the jack on my desk.

"I wonder if you wouldn't mind helping me find some photos from your childhood. You can even include some with your mom in them, if you'd like. We're making a slideshow for the birthday party, and it will not be complete without including some of your pictures."

"I have a nail appointment in an hour." I stepped over the two discarded sweaters on the floor and crossed to the closet and fingered a short leather coat. *No, too warm.*

She followed. "I understand you're busy, but what about the pictures?"

I didn't answer, but instead, I walked around her to the mirror and stared at my sullen expression. I wanted her to go away. But she didn't. "I'll see what I can do."

"I appreciate that." Meredith still didn't leave, but instead remained in the doorway, blocking my path to freedom.

"What?" I snapped.

"We are having dinner tonight. I really would love to have you here. It would be a chance for us to get to know each other better, just the four of us."

I glowered at her in the mirror. *Get to know each*

25

other better? Why would I want to do that? But I knew she would not shoo until I agreed. "Sure. I'll be here."

Meredith smiled. "Wonderful. Six o'clock sharp." She patted my shoulder and sauntered back down the hall.

I rolled my eyes, folded to the carpet next to my bed, and peered underneath. The round flowered box, filled with my mother's pictures, sat hidden just out of reach. I leaned forward and scooped it out. Dust powdered the top. How long had it been since I dared open it? I stared at the box a moment, unsure if I should open it now.

Skittles rushed the box and batted at the string that tied it closed.

I let her tug on it until it came undone. She smacked it a few more times, then got distracted by a fly and scurried off.

Now untied, I raised a manicured finger to the lid and tipped it over. The top tumbled to the carpet, and I peered inside. Mounds of photos lay on one another, all sizes and shapes—some snapshots, some digital prints, others department store specials. One of the three of us, a few months before she died, rested at the top of the stack. A few of Mom being silly for the camera made me smile. But my favorite was a candid shot of her and Dad holding me as a baby. Enormous redwood trees filled the background, making my parents look diminutive in size. No matter how stunning the scenery, none of it compared to her beauty. Golden hair, big, almond-shaped green eyes, smooth ivory skin—Dad spoke the truth, we resembled each other some. Well, back before I dyed my hair the color of the week. I touched my blue, textured bob and frowned. It in no way mirrored her gorgeous, model-like wavy hair.

I stroked a finger down her photographed mane. "I was better with you here, Mom." A tear escaped, and I batted at it with annoyance.

The silhouette of the maid appeared in my doorway.

"What, Anastasia?" I rammed the lid back onto the box, leapt to my feet, and kicked the pictures back under the bed.

"My name's Eunice, ma'am," she said. "I have your tea."

"I've renamed you Anastasia. Better, don't you think? Of course, that's hard to say. Too long. I shall call you Ana for short." I walked back to the closet, stepped into some red pumps, and vamped in the mirror. My eyes appeared puffy and bloodshot. *Great. I'll have to fix my makeup in the car.* "I need you to contact my hairdresser. I can't go to the party with faded blue tips, now can I?"

"No, ma'am, I suppose not." She held out a tray. "Your tea. Where would you like it?"

"No time for tea, Ana." I stuffed my phone into a red purse and swung the strap over my shoulder. "Now call the limo. I need to get going."

"He's already in front."

"Awesome." I sauntered down the large staircase and out the door.

The limo driver's gaze met mine, and he smiled.

My heart skipped. His brown eyes and gleaming smile looked amazing against his bronzed skin. If only he wasn't an insignificant servant.

"Are you okay?" he asked.

I startled, then blinked "Are you new, driver?"

27

"Yes," he said with a deep and husky voice. "I'm Henry. A friend of a friend got me this job."

I stared with narrowed eyes and a tight smile. Did it matter he was completely gorgeous? *Maybe...Nope. Still poor.* I slipped my sunglasses on and folded my arms. "Well, your friend of a friend doesn't get any points with me. You're not very good."

"Excuse me?" He scowled.

"I'm still standing here on the curb." I gestured toward the closed car door. "Hel-lo. The door, driver."

"Oh." He blinked, then rushed to open it, and stepped back. "Sorry, ma'am."

I slid in and peered back over my sunglasses. "And in the future, don't address me unless I address you firs—"

The door slammed shut. I pursed my lips. He'd pay for that later.

Chapter Five

The club reverberated with techno sounds. Laser lights of all colors danced to the beat, crisp in the smoke-filled air. People gyrated in rhythmic flow, drinking, laughing, and yelling to converse. I weaved through the sweaty, swaying bodies to the bar.

The bartender leaned over. "What are you having?"

"A purple passion," I screamed back.

He nodded, snatched a glass from a stack, spun it through his fingers, and landed it on the block in one fluid motion. He grabbed two bottles by their necks, one with clear liquid, another with grape juice, and mixed them in the glass. Next, he sprayed it with seltzer water, dropped a cherry inside, and then slid the tumbler across to me.

I handed him a twenty-dollar bill across the counter. "Keep it." Then I winked and turned to the room. The cell phone in my back pocket buzzed for the incessant sixth or seventh time. I gave in and glanced at the screen:

—*Where are you? Remember, we're having dinner together.*—

Meredith. I groaned. No way did I feel like going home right now—especially to her. This morning shook me a bit. I should never have let myself feel something. I knew better. Stay out of the past. It hurt too much. Live for the now. Only do what made me happy.

29

Meredith did not make me happy. Like a designer knock-off, she could not be a real replacement for something I loved.

Dad could have had any woman, and who did he pick? A hippie, part-time waitress at a local greasy spoon diner in the lower-east end of Los Angeles. How trite. Single mom, clearly hurting for money, flirting with a newly widowed man. Disgusting. Shame on her. I laid the phone facedown on the counter and glanced at the fairly attractive guy sliding toward me. With a flick of his head, he sent dark bangs out of his face, revealing two chocolate-brown eyes at half-mast. I let my stare travel down to his chiseled abs clearly visible through his taut black T-shirt.

"Hi," he said.

"Hi, yourself." I kept my gaze over the rim of the glass, as I sipped the drink in my hand.

"What are you having?" he slurred.

"Whatever you want to buy me." I grinned a seductive smile, setting the empty tumbler onto the counter.

He turned and waved to the bartender. "Two Tom Collins, please."

"Good choice." I leaned into him and smiled.

A different bartender walked up this time and glowered. "ID."

I reached into my purse and plucked out my fake driver's license. I had to do a lot of flirting to get this card, but some nerd actually bought that I'd hang out with him if he got it for me. Never did. Don't need to. Besides, I'd be twenty-one soon. Like anything would change in that amount of time. I'd still be the same person—lonely and sad, in need of a drink.

The husky bartender glanced at it, then walked away, returning with two tall, clear glasses, topped them with a lime, and slid them across the counter.

The guy paid, then leaned on his elbow. "I'm Pete."

"Thanks for the drink, Pete." I blew a kiss at his cheek, rose from the stool, and sauntered away. I sensed his stare burning into my back, but I wouldn't give him the satisfaction of turning around. I swallowed until the glass became empty, and then tricked another guy into another one. Of course, I could easily pay for my own drinks. After all, I had a few $100 bills tucked in my purse, but where was the fun in that?

I squeezed between a couple of brothers on a couch and smiled at each of them. They, of course, bought me a few rounds of whiskey sours. My head whirled, the room swayed below my feet, but another guy across the room motioned with a wave of a finger to join him. I allowed him to buy me a beer. I chased that down with another shot of something gross that burned my throat. At this point, my legs wavered beneath me, and I struggled to remain vertical. But my thoughts had finally numbed. No more pain, which was the way I liked it.

My phone buzzed in my pocket again. I held the screen close, squinted, and read, *Dad*. With some effort, I stumbled to the restroom with the floor blurring and swaying, to finally answer it. "Hi, Dad. What's up?" I slurred.

"Where are you, Cynthia?"

"Out."

"Meredith said she is worried sick. You were supposed to be home hours ago."

I rolled my eyes. "I'm fine."

"Where are you?"

"The Generation's Bar on Fourth." I slapped a hand over my mouth, then mouthed, *Shoot!"*

"Bar? Cindy, you're only twenty."

"Don't worry; they wouldn't let me in," I lied.

"I'm sending a limo. You better take it."

"Yes, sir." I saluted the air.

"I'm warning you, Cynthia."

"I see that. Look, I am an adult and—"

The line cut dead.

"Dad?" I blew through my lips. *Real nice, Dad. Hang up. Super mature.* "And you think I'm the childish one?" I staggered back through the crowd and out to the parking lot. A blast of cool air licked my damp skin, and I regretted not bringing a jacket. Of course, I usually didn't. They concealed my curves, and I detested carrying them.

A valet started to approach me, but I held up a hand. "Back off, dude. My limo is coming."

The guy shook his head and crossed back to the booth.

Suddenly, the ground shifted beneath my weight. My head swirled in indistinct colors. Nausea surged through my stomach. I cringed at the burning poison in my throat. I swallowed against the bile and begged my body not to puke. I despised vomiting. Especially when it got in my hair. So gross. I leaned my forehead against the building, hoping to still the world beneath my feet.

The club door opened behind me, sending music and joviality pouring out for a moment. I peered to the side at whoever had exited the building and frowned.

Pete staggered straight for me. Too drunk to

escape, he drew alongside my cheek and murmured, "So, you like to trick men into paying for your drinks, huh?"

The stench of sweat and alcohol permeated my nose, and I swallowed not to gag. "Why not?" I laughed, flipping away.

He shuffled around to the front of me and brought an arm to the wall by my face.

Suddenly, my tummy curdled. Burning stomach acid mixed with too many drinks and a handful of nuts spewed from my mouth to his feet.

He jumped back, eyes wide, then they tapered. He stepped over the mess and grabbed my wrist, hard.

My heart accelerated. I shook my arm to wrench free, but my muscles were too weak in their drunken state to do any good. "Let go! You're hurting me."

"Good. Maybe you'll think twice next time." He yanked me toward him.

Unable to balance, I fell into his chest.

His free hand traveled down my body.

Panicked, I opened my mouth to yell.

He clamped his hand over my lips.

I couldn't breathe. I called him names, muffled by his hand.

He hissed in my ear, "Shut up, or—"

Someone yanked me back and punched Pete's jaw, sending him sprawling hard to the cement.

Blood trickled from a slight cut on the drunk guy's upper lip. He glanced up, mouth open, eyes wide.

My hero leveled a foot taller than Pete and had at least twenty pounds more muscle. This would not be a fair fight. The dude must have come to the same conclusion because he scrambled backward, up, and staggered back inside the building without another word or glance back.

My knight turned around.

I frowned. Of course, it had to be the new limo driver.

He held out a hand. "You okay?"

"Fine," I snapped, more embarrassed than anything. I took his hand to stand, then jerked it back, toppled toward the long car, and waited for him to open the door.

He let out audible sigh, then crossed to let me in.

As the door closed, I heard him mutter, "Thank you, Henry."

"Why should I have to say thank you? Just do your job." I lay back on the seat and closed my eyes, wanting to sleep forever.

Chapter Six

Half awake, half asleep, I allowed distant memories to surface of my mother and the last time I saw her. The saddest thing? I liked who I was with her. I liked us—our family. Why did she have to go? Now, love escaped me—from others to myself. No one, not even Dad, could comfort my broken psyche. I knew nothing about me felt pleasant. I hated myself. Why would anyone else care? Not that I wanted them to. I had learned to live with my misery. So, if I had to be miserable, why should I let anyone else off the hook?

I rolled over in the bed and tried to push the sad memories away. I lifted the satin sleeping mask from my face. The morning light blinded me, so I snapped it back on, but not before catching a glimpse of Charlotte and Gabby standing at the foot of my bed. I really did not want to see them right now. "Go away."

"We can't," came Gabby's voice.

"Sure, you can. Face the door, walk toward it, and leave out of it. Easy peesy."

"We're on a mission," Charlotte said.

The bed jiggled, and I assumed one of them now sat on my mattress. "I don't care. I'm sleeping." I rolled over and tucked my comforter tighter under my chin to demonstrate my point.

"We aren't leaving until you hear us out."

I'm not sure which one said that, but I felt the

pressure of both of them pushing in on my sides. "Fine!" I flipped down the comforter. "What do you want?"

"You missed Mom's dinner last night," Gabby said. "We wanted to talk to you about that."

I lifted the mask to peek out again. Gabby's strawberry hair frizzed dreadfully in the air, but in some weird way, it matched her prolonged nose and freckles. Put a black pointy hat on her, and she'd be the perfect witch for Halloween. I turned away with an exaggerated sigh.

"She had some good news to share, too." Gabby shuffled around to the other side of the bed and leaned in.

Her breath smelled of stale coffee and peanut butter. *Gross.* I covered my face with the pillow and exhaled with a humph, hoping they could sense my exasperation and leave.

"Don't you want to know what it is?" came Charlotte's annoying shriek on the other side of me.

Not really. I needed more sleep. To detox from the alcohol still lingering in my system, but more importantly from the past memories that made me spiral into a place of depression. I refused to fall into that state again. I needed to sleep these emotions away.

Gabby squatted by my side and peered between the pillow and mattress, so that her nose came into view. "We got a puppy. Isn't that great?"

"That's great," I said dryly. "One more mouth for my dad to feed." I tugged the pillow tighter. *Please leave.*

"Also, Mom, sent us in here because we need some pictures for your dad's slide show. Do you think you could find us some, please?"

"Go away."

Charlotte touched my calf.

I hurled my leg away, slammed my back up against the headboard, and yanked off my mask. "Do not touch me! Ever!"

Charlotte's green eyes broadened as her palms lifted. "Sorry, I just…we need…"

"We need those pictures today," Gabby said. "The party is on—"

"Look, I know when his party is. I will get the pictures when I'm good and ready to, *capisce*?" I glared at her a long moment. "Now scram. You're both messing with my routine."

"You promise, you'll get us the pictures?" Gabby dared to ask again.

"Yes, now scram!"

Both scampered out of the room, probably off to cry.

I didn't ask for sisters. Being an only child suited me just fine. Siblings complicated things. Sharing Dad would never be okay. Especially with those two. Worst choice ever. I had known the sisters since grade school—super nerdy, they had always dressed weird, and continually said the most awkward comments in class. Most people made fun of them. Sure, I used to be nice to them, but not after their mom wiggled into my home. Now, they just annoyed me. I didn't need sisters or friends. I wanted to be left alone. Was that too much to ask?

Skittles leapt into my lap and wiggled her body into the curve of my thigh in the comforter. I stroked her fur, and she responded by purring. "Okay, I'm lying," I whispered to her fuzzy ear. Who didn't want friends? If I reflected honestly, a part of me felt bad about the way I treated those two girls. But my heart hurt too much to go there. I couldn't forgive their family for moving into mine. Not yet...maybe not ever.

The maid cleared her throat in the doorway. "Miss, just a reminder that your hair appointment is in an hour."

I yawned and slid to the edge of the bed.

She turned to go.

"Ana."

The woman pivoted back around; her lips pressed together. "Miss?"

"Did the cook make any baked goods this morning?"

"Yes."

"What kind?"

"Orange cranberry scones."

"Awesome. Please have a coffee, the way I like it, and a scone waiting at the door in about thirty minutes."

"Yes, miss." She hurried away.

Probably before I could ask for more. I usually did, which made me smile. I felt incredibly ornery this morning. I sighed and shuffled to the restroom.

After a quick shower and a tour of my closet, I sauntered down the stairs in true artistic form. No mystery, I rocked my new designer, cream-colored dress and cheetah heels. I had just reached the bottom stair, when I overheard Meredith talking to Dad on speaker phone.

"She totally blew me off yesterday, Jack. Not to mention, she got home sometime after midnight, totally drunk out of her mind."

"Are you sure?" came Dad's voice.

"Yes, she stumbled up the stairs all the way to her room. Look, I won't have her influencing my girls this way. You have to do something about her, or she is going to destroy this family."

Too late. You already destroyed this family, I thought before bolting to the entrance and slamming the door behind me. How dare she tattle on me—to *my* father. That woman had been a pain in my side from the minute she came into our lives. I glanced around the empty driveway. *Great.* The limo wasn't parked in front; I would have to drive myself. Normally, I wouldn't have minded, but right now, my thoughts whirled, and my emotions surged out of control. I just wanted to close my eyes and make the world reset to some sort of sanity.

The front door opened behind me. The maid held out a lunch bag and coffee cup.

I rolled my eyes, ripped them out of her hands, and stormed off to my black sports car. I placed the bag on the roof, dug my keys out of my purse, and clicked the remote to get in. Stupid Meredith. Why did she have to be here? I wanted my mom back so badly. I hated that my reality had come crashing to this point.

I detested who she made me. A wench with a hardened heart that might never heal. I feared I would be a monster forever. Each encounter made it worse. Every day I became a little more awful. I knew it. But it played like a movie outside my body. I could not curb my evil thoughts. I could not stop my rage. My wicked actions overtook me again and again. No one truly wanted to be this cruel, unless she had some sort of psychotic condition. *Did I? Am I insane?* I closed my eyes and exhaled out all my air until it hurt.

A twig fell from a nearby tree onto my car's roof and startled me. A few tears had escaped down my cheeks. I had cried more in the last twenty-four hours than I had in years. It irritated me.

I flipped down the mirror on my car visor and dabbed at my damp eyes. One drop had lined my makeup and left a black smudge on my right cheek. I had to stop thinking about this stuff. I had suppressed these memories for a darn good reason. Why were they coming back? I did not want this. I needed to forget—to be lost in some boy's arms or in the bottom of a bottle. I slammed the visor up, jammed the key in the ignition, and twisted it. The engine roared to life. I squealed out of the parking lot, determined to ignore the past, and be lost in the now.

Chapter Seven

I sauntered through the department store, petting rows of scarves and bracelets. Women in designer suits and painted faces helped other women carry clothes to the dressing rooms or brought them an espresso. Twice I had been approached, but I waved them off. I didn't want to be pampered. I wanted to be left alone to achieve my mission.

A turquoise scarf with yellow daisies laid folded on a table. Without continuing to eye it, I tucked it neatly into the designer purse I had selected a few racks back. Of course, I had the money to buy both the scarf and the bag, but after feeling dead for days, stealing pumped adrenaline into my veins. My senses jolted alive, and for the moment, I could breathe again. I fingered a silver cuff and folded it back into the leather pocket.

Passing the cosmetic counter, I lifted a sample perfume and powder. Without pausing, I stepped through the doorway, and an alarm sounded above. I did not halt. Instead, I rushed faster toward my car. A new state law prevented the store employees from following customers into the parking lot.

As soon as I left the store, freedom followed me. Some stupid government official totally ruled in my favor. I often marveled at how absurd our society had become, with rules in favor of the criminal. *Brilliant*.

But in this minute, I praised their stupidity. I sprang into my car and drove down the street, entering traffic, super proud of what I had just accomplished.

On the corner, a haggard woman, probably in her late forties, panhandled in ripped sweats and a stained T-shirt. Her matted hair was partially covered by a blue beanie. In her hand, she held a cardboard sign that read, *Will eat for food.*

The sign amused me, which little did these days. I reached in my purse, lifted out a perfume and the scarf, and handed them out. "Have a lovely day."

"Thank you," she said.

The light turned green, and I hit the gas and floored it through the intersection. Fifteen minutes later, I parked in the circular driveway and shut off the car. The engine ticked in the cool autumn air. From the driver's seat, I leaned my head sideways to stare up at the two-story mansion. The curved adobe front with rust-colored clay tiles—my mom's favorite attribute—now only brought sadness. Having been born in Spain, Mom said the Spanish architecture made her feel at home. But it wasn't her home anymore, was it? And it didn't feel like mine, either.

I slid out of the car, slammed the door, and strolled up the front steps. A soft breeze blew through the air, sending dried leaves skittering across the steps behind me. For a moment, I waited in front of the carved wooden doors, not wanting to go in. Though exciting for the moment, shoplifting had not released the pain deep inside. I did not want to stay here. I would change and go out to party. After a few drinks, all memories would be obliterated. This place, the women who defiled it, the absence of my father, the loss of my mother, and the constant loneliness—all of it. Poof! Gone at the bottom of an empty glass.

I turned the knob, opened the door, and cringed. Tweedledee and Tweedledumb bounded down the stairway, straight for me, with obnoxiously huge grins.

"Oh, good, you're home." Charlotte giggled and clapped her hands. "We've been waiting for you to get here. Mom has been trying to get a hold of you."

"Yeah, what's new?" I pushed past them. The girls trailed me up the stairs nipping at my heels. So insufferable. *Go away!*

"You really should answer your cell phone, Cindy. I think it's bad. You should talk to her," Gabby said.

I stopped and exhaled loudly to make sure they grasped my frustration. "Look, I don't care about *your* mom. I don't care about *you*. I barely care about myself. I just want to be left alone. So, please, for the love of all chocolate, Hollywood, and social media, leave me be." I turned back and finished my trek to my room, this time unaccompanied.

Inside, I dropped face-first to my comforter and closed my eyes. My body relaxed. I'd about dozed off, when I heard my bedroom door creak open.

"Cindy," came Meredith's distinct smooth voice.

I gave a slight snore, pretending to be asleep.

"I know you're awake." Her voice came from the side of my bed. "The police just called. They said you were shoplifting at Darren's this afternoon."

I peeked out one lid, then pushed my back against the headboard. "How do they know it was me?"

"You've been in magazines before. It's not like you're an unknown."

I shrugged. "So? Dad will make it disappear. He

43

always does."

"Maybe, maybe not, but you can't keep living like this. You're hurting your dad." She let out a deep sigh. "Which means you are hurting all of us."

"Us?" I sneered. A lecture from this woman hurt worse than pouring rubbing alcohol on an open wound. "You're not my mother, Meredith."

"No, you're right. I'm not. Because if I were, I would severely punish you for the rest of your life. Your dad is way too soft."

I stared at her sullen expression. *What happened to all the sunshine and roses?* Meredith pretended to be so sweet, but deep down I knew all along—the true her. If she kept it up, I would finally have the proof I needed— the evil stepmother.

"I have a message from your father," she said.

Since when did Dad relay messages through her to me?

"Your father said his threat is real, and he will implement it when he returns. He said, you'd know what that meant."

I smiled a tight, sarcastic grin. "Great. Can't wait. Thanks."

Meredith gaped for a moment.

I detected no anger in her eyes, only pain. But I could not let myself care about this woman. Not for a second. I would not allow myself, under any circumstances, to start feeling anything for her. Not even if my actions caused her discomfort. The mysterious "they" could call me cold and heartless; I didn't care. It was the way it was. It needed to stay that way. "Is that all?" I snapped.

"You know, Cindy. I never wanted to replace your

mom. I only ever wanted to be your friend," she said, her tone softer.

"Haven't you noticed, Meredith? I don't have friends." I slithered back down under the comforter and rolled away.

"That's a sad way to live," Meredith whispered.

"Maybe so, but it's my life." After a long pause, I wondered if she had left. I flipped over and saw she still waited, hands folded, waiting for something. "What?" I asked, annoyed.

"I know you have no desire to help me," she said, "but could you please help do something nice for your father? I would like some pictures for the birthday slideshow."

Exhaustion assaulted every muscle in my body. I could not fight this anymore. Obviously, this woman would not go away unless I gave her what she wanted. I pivoted slightly onto my back and pointed down over the side of the mattress. "Round box under my bed."

She knelt onto the floor, lifted the comforter slightly, and withdrew the flowered box.

The sight of her holding my mother's memories hurt my heart, but I could not battle any longer. It didn't matter anymore anyways.

"Thank you. I'll return them after the party on Friday night." She crossed to the door, then looked back. "Cindy, I really hope something changes. I see you going down an extremely dark path, and I'm afraid of what's on the other side."

I closed my eyes to indicate the end of the conversation. A moment later, I heard the snap of her sandals fade down the hall. I flipped to my back and stared at the high, textured ceiling. I don't know how long I lay like that, but my mood did not improve.

Chapter Eight

Cars started to arrive around seven p.m.—vehicles that cost six digits all lined up in the driveway to celebrate Dad's birthday ball. Sure, it was my celebration, too, but they weren't here for me. The roar of conversation, the clink of glasses, and the occasional laugh filtered from below. I needed to hurry. Dad would be waiting for me to arrive.

I pivoted back and forth in front of my floor-length mirror for one final check. My freshly dyed, platinum-blonde hair with no more hints of blue, laid soft and wavy to my jawline. I liked the layers. Though I would never tell my hairdresser, Maria, she had done an excellent job on my cut. Edgy, but cute. I nudged a strand back behind one ear, revealing a diamond stud. A gift for graduating high school from Dad. I traveled my gaze down my reflection. The light-blue gown lay slightly off the shoulder and hugged my waist nicely, before spanning out at the hips to the floor. Like a small girl, I swayed side to side to hear the swish. I reached for Mom's crystal tiara and placed it on my head. A simple hairpiece instantly transformed me into a fairytale princess. Mom would have loved it. I batted those thoughts away, not wanting to dwell on that right now. I slid on some rhinestone-glass stilettos, caught one more glimpse of myself in the mirror, and then sauntered out my bedroom door.

Once in the backyard, the crowd drew me in. Designer suits and name-brand dresses, necks dripping with diamond and pearls, all denoted big bank accounts and influential status. Most conversations dwelled on investments, real estate, charity events, and travel. Every once in a while, I heard movie project or actor pitches. This was Hollywood—everyone was only as big as his or her last job. And everyone wanted to be rich and famous.

"Cynthia?" I heard someone say my name. I spun around and frowned at the sight of the washed-up actress—so washed up, I couldn't even remember her name. She did a few projects with Dad several years ago, but she had a bad attitude, so my father blackballed her from the industry. So goes the life of a diva. Her purpose for being here crystal clear—to win back Dad's affection. *Good luck.*

"You've grown up so gorgeous," she purred.

I narrowed my eyes. "How did you get on the guest list? Didn't my dad fire you?"

She pinched her lips and didn't reply.

"That's what I thought." I rolled my eyes and continued through the herd of socialites in search of the "birthday boy." A few more people nodded at me as I passed, but most turned away. Not surprising. I had been wicked to a lot of the people here. I couldn't help it. They all wanted something from my father—a huge pet peeve of mine. No one came to these things for the love of birthday cake and Dad. A bunch of fake friends and moochers. They all repulsed me. As a lead producer in Hollywood, Dad had money, power, and influence. Everyone knew it. And everyone wanted it. If he lost it all, they'd disappear in a blink of an eye. So, who could blame me for being a little rude sometimes?

Across the lawn, I spotted Dad. He conversed with a few men next to a three-tiered level of white buttercream frosting adorned with gold leaf and silver balls. As I got closer, I could make out the gold writing with the words, *Happy Birthday, Jack and Cindy*. Underneath the décor, likely our favorite—red velvet. His gaze met mine, and I waved and smiled.

He waved but did not return my grin.

Odd. He always smiled at me. "Happy birthday, Dad," I said once I reached him.

"Excuse me," he said to a man next to him and motioned with the crook of his finger for me to follow him to the side of the garden behind a tall hedge. Once there, he faced me, his expression tense. "I heard you were not good while I was away."

"I promise, I tried." I faked a pout.

"I've had it with you," his voice stayed to a terse whisper, "I meant it when I said you needed to be nicer to the servants, the family, and that you would need to look for a job or else. Did you think I was joking about all of that?"

"Sort of." I giggled.

The vein in his neck pulsed. "I honestly do not know what to do with you anymore, Cynthia. I've had it."

"Dad, please. I haven't seen you in almost a week." I held out my arms for a hug.

But he stepped back instead.

Why was he acting like this? It confused me. Hurt even. "Come on, Dad. It's our birthday. Can't we talk about this later? I know you want to have a good time. So do I. Let's just—"

"No!" He thrust his finger at the air in front of me. "I meant everything I said before I left. I told you what I wanted for my birthday. Honestly, it is *all* I want."

Tears pooled in my eyes. He had no idea what I went through. He only cared about whether or not I treated the servants and Meredith nice. But what about me? Couldn't he see his broken daughter? Completely lost and alone. That right now, all I wanted was for Dad to hug me and tell me everything would be okay.

"Crying will not change any of this. Whatever happens from here on out is your fault!" He stormed around the hedge and back to the party.

I dropped onto a nearby stone bench, troubled, confused, and afraid. Ignoring my perfect makeup, I allowed myself to cry. Losing him would destroy me. He was it. He was all I cared about—all I had left.

The crowd began to sing, "Happy Birthday."

I dabbed at my tears with my wrist, rolled my shoulders back, and strode around the bush barricade. The crowd thickened toward the front. I tried to shove through, but no one would get out of the way. Didn't they understand? I had to stand next to him. Today was *our* birthday. Since before I could walk, it had been our tradition for us to blow out the candles together. I shifted past a few more people. "Please, I need to get to my dad." I figured, as soon as he saw me, he'd beckon me forward. "Excuse me," I said to a lady who had linked arms with some guy.

She glanced at me but didn't budge.

I squeezed between her and a kid. As I neared the front, Dad came into view.

Meredith positioned on one side, her daughters on his other side.

The candles glowed against his face.

I lifted my hand to let him know I was there, but he didn't look up.

Instead, he puckered his lips, paused for a wish, and blew. The flames dissipated into smoldering wicks.

Everyone clapped and cheered.

All but me. Frozen, still a few feet away, unable to comprehend what had just occurred.

Dad hugged his new wife and her two girls. He did not seek me out.

In that moment, I understood. I had been replaced. Complete clarity slammed into my chest—I had no one. Surrounded by fifty people, I felt completely isolated. Tears burned my eyes. I sprinted through the crowd, knocking people out of the way as I went. A few cussed at me, but I didn't care. I had to go. Anywhere but here.

As I approached the limo, Henry didn't talk this time; he opened the door and stepped aside. *Better. He can be taught.* I glided in.

He slammed the door closed without any acknowledgement.

I glanced up and about jumped through the roof. "What the—?"

An elderly woman dressed in a form-fitting white pantsuit sat across from me. Her salty black-and-gray hair laid piled high on her head in rose-shaped swirls. Though she seemed old, her dark skin looked radiant, smooth, flawless with golden shades of makeup that seemed to glow.

"Who are you?" I asked.

She smiled. "We'll get to that."

I frantically hit the button for the divider, but it wouldn't go down. I tried the door, but it also did not work. "What's going on? What are you doing in my limo?"

"We'll get to that. Right now, you just need to shut up and listen." Her voice sounded melodic, calm.

"I'm sorry, what?" How dare she talk to me like that. I sat taller, ready to pounce. "I don't *need* to do anything. Especially with you." I dug around in my clutch purse for my phone.

The woman held up a manicured hand to study her long, gold nails. "You are sorry. A sorry excuse for a human being. I would say you need a lot more than I can probably give you."

"What do you want? Are you a struggling actress who thinks I can influence my dad for you? Forget it. Not happening."

"I'm not an actress."

"Then what are you...poor?" I shook my head. "Well, I don't do handouts. We're not giving you a dime."

"You might have all the money in the world—well, did anyway—but there is nothing you have that I would want, dear. Your soul is at a complete deficit, and you are, therefore, insignificant."

"Huh! I'm worth more than you, I can promise you that." Furious, I rammed the button on the armrest over and over with my finger, then my fist. "Come on!" It would not budge. I yanked the door, kicked it, punched it, and jerked it. *Why won't it open?* I cursed, then snapped, "Do you know who I am?"

"Awe, yes. The infamous question all spoiled, rich brats ask when they somehow think they are entitled to more than they are." She sat forward with a plastic smile that did not match her narrowed, incensed eyes.

"You are Cynthia Tremaine. Born twenty-one years ago tomorrow to Jack Tremaine and a woman that I dare say, you did not deserve to have as a mother. You are spoiled, pretentious, and mostly ridiculous. Yeah, I know who you are, doll. And I am not impressed in the least."

"Excuse me!"

"There is no excuse for you...well, your actions anyway."

Lava gushed through my blood stream. Frantically, I shoved and kicked the door. Nothing. Solid, unmoving. I kicked it a few more times to no avail. I was seconds away from striking the window with the heel of my shoe. "Are you friends with the limo driver? Because he's soooo fired."

Her expression remained stoic as she slid forward with a sly smirk. "Oh, no, oh wretched one. I am your fairy godmother."

I laughed. "Wow, I don't remember doing any drugs, but you never know."

She snapped her fingers, and the divider moved down and then up. She snapped again, and the door unlocked.

I reached for the handle.

But the woman snapped again, and it sealed shut.

Hallucinations. What was happening? I rubbed my eyes and shook my head side to side. Someone must have put something in my drink. I just didn't remember having one yet.

"The sooner you accept this, the sooner we can get on with it."

Has to be a dream. Maybe I still slept in my bed. I squeezed my eyes shut, then peeked through my lashes.

The woman waved.

I tried again. The same thing happened. Giving up, I opened my eyes, crossed my arms, and glared. *Fine.* Better play along, get this over with, so she'd get out of my limo, and I could get to the bar. "Okay, you're my fairy godmother. Are you here to make me a princess?"

"While some women deserve to be princesses, well, some deserve to be maids." She smiled an obnoxious grin.

It was the kind of sneer I gave women I didn't really like but wanted to belittle. "This is pointless. Whoever put you up to this is so dead." I rolled my eyes. "We all know which I deserve."

"Yes, dear. We all know which you deserve."

"So, who put you up to this?"

"A simple birthday wish, oh rancid one. Just a simple blow of the candles, and poof, here I am. Ready to change your destiny."

"Birthday wish?" That landed like a kick in my stomach. "My dad? There was no way he would wish this." Or would he?

"Um, I'm afraid it's all he wanted. Do you not listen to anyone but yourself? He said it like half-a-dozen times."

I stared, not sure what to say.

She folded her hands and shifted forward in the seat. "Listen to me closely, Miss Tremaine. If you do not accept what is about to happen to you, if you fight this, if you ignore any lesson that might be learned, it will become permanent. Do you understand? So, be a good, little Cindy, and do what you're told. Evolve. Morph. Become something"—she waved a hand over the space in front of me with a disgusted expression—

"anything better than this."

"I'm sorry, but people don't talk to me like that."

"Maybe they should," she sneered. "Now hush, I wasn't finished. Hasn't anyone ever told you that it's impolite to interrupt someone when she is talking?"

My eyes widened, my nostrils flared, and my lips puckered. Fast, rapid breaths pressed from my lungs. I wanted to punch this woman, but I would likely break a nail. Or worse, sprain my wrist. It happened to a girl in high school when she slapped some guy. Violence wasn't really my thing, anyway, but for this woman, I could make an exception.

"The only way to get out of what's about to happen to you is to change. Seriously change. You need to show you've become a better person by the stroke of midnight on New Year's Eve. If that doesn't happen, well, let's just say you will not be happy with the outcome, my dear putrid. Do you understand?" She held up a red, bedazzled cell phone.

My cell phone! "Hey, where did you get that?" I leapt forward to grab it.

But she pushed me back with her foot. "Not important." She glanced at the screen. "Oh, wow, time flies. Almost midnight now. I don't want to turn into a pumpkin. Must be flying, kind of like this cell phone." She snapped, and the skylight slid open. She chucked the phone out the gap. A splash could be heard at the fountain nearby.

"Are you crazy?" I grabbed the handle on the door and jiggled it with all my might, unsuccessfully. I dropped to my knees, crawled to the skylight, stood on my tiptoes, and faced the fountain. The one lamppost did little to light the driveway, and I couldn't see anything. I knelt back, but the woman had disappeared. *Good riddance.* I tried the door again. It didn't budge. I slipped back into the opening in the roof, placed my elbows on the edge, and propelled myself up and out. I scraped my thigh on the edge of the opening and cursed. I would get even with this woman. *So, help me.* Well, as soon as I found out who she was.

I slid down from the top over the back window, to the trunk, and onto the driveway. Not an easy task. Once standing, I ran in the direction she had tossed my phone. It lay at the bottom of the fountain. I tossed out a few more choice words, leaned forward, and scooped it out of the water. The cracked display bubbled underneath and would no longer turn on. *Wait until Dad hears about this.* I glanced around the circular driveway but saw no one. All the cars had left. I walked toward the house and tripped on something. I hit the ground hard.

"Ouch!" My hand stung from scraping against the brick. I pushed back up and brushed off my dress, then gasped at the rough cotton material. *What am I wearing?* I glanced in the limo window, and my vision blurred with stars. The reflection revealed a gray maid's uniform. *Gross.* I turned and tripped again. What was my problem? I glanced down and gasped. My sparkly rhinestone-glass heels had been replaced by tan canvas slip-ons one can find at any bargain basement. *Doubly gross.* Someone needed to wake me up from this nightmare.

I stumbled forward to the driver's side and peeked in. Vacant. I walked around the corner of the mansion. Not a soul in the backyard. Weird. When did all the party guests leave? How long was I in that car anyhow?

In the distance, a siren sounded. Red and blue lights flashed just outside the entrance. The main gate slid open, and a black-and-white car sped in.

Perfect timing. Now, I could report that woman. With her voodoo magic, she had somehow managed to steal my dress, my shoes, and... I touched my head and hmphed. And my tiara. That was from my mother. Now the old fairy fart-mother was truly going down. I walked around to the front, ready to complain.

The cop car halted within inches of my feet, forcing me to jump back. "What the heck, dude?" I screamed as the driver's door opened. "You could have hit me."

A corpulent man in a brown uniform stepped out with a solemn expression. His handlebar mustache twitched to the side. "Are you Cynthia Taylor?"

"Tremaine. In the flesh," I said annoyed, then changed my tune. "Look, I'm glad you're here. There was this woman who broke into my limo and stole my—"

"You're under arrest."

I laughed. "Funny."

The cop put a hand on his weapon and approached me. "Put your hands on the side of my car and spread your legs."

"Yeah, right." I stepped back. "In your dreams, moron."

"Don't make me say it again. Hands against the front of my car, now!"

"For what?" I asked, not amused. First, that old lady destroyed my phone and now, this cop. "Whoever set me up, tell them I'm officially punked, and let's call it a day. Okay? I'm sure this will go viral. Who is filming?" I glanced around. "Good for you. Enough though. I'm exhausted." I turned for the house.

In a fluid motion, the policeman caught my wrist, propelled me forward, and pinned me hard against the back of his car.

Pain shot through my chest. I didn't have a ton up-front, but I had enough that slamming my "girls" against the hood stung a bit. "Take it easy. That hurt."

"You're under arrest for shoplifting at Darren's Department Store. You have the right to remain silent. Anything you say can and will be used against you in a court of law. You have the right to have an attorney present. If you do not have the ability to obtain an attorney, you may have one appointed to you. Do you understand these rights as I have explained them to you?" the cop asked.

"You aren't serious?"

"Do you understand these rights?"

Perhaps I needed to handle this a bit more politically. "Surely, we can do something to work this out, officer," I purred.

"Do you understand these rights as I have stated them?"

The clanking of handcuffs sounded behind me, then they pinched at my wrists. "Do you know who my father is?" I yelled. "He'll have your badge for this." The cop ignored my rant and tossed me in the back of his grimy car where I'm sure drug addicts and prostitutes had probably oozed filth. No shower would get these germs off my body. That was for sure.

He climbed into the car and turned off the lights.

"Do you understand how in trouble you are, mister?" I leaned forward to the crisscross bars between us. "My dad is Jack Tremaine. I'm sure you've heard of him. He's like one of the biggest movie producers in Hollywood. He made like forty blockbusters and is Tinsel Town's most sought-after guy right now. People do favors for him, you know. You understand what that means, right? People will take care of his problem for a price." I dropped back against the seat and narrowed my eyes at his reflection in the rearview mirror. "You could benefit, or you can be a dead man."

No response.

"You're so dead. I do not envy you."

Still without a word, the cop drove out of the driveway.

"Do you understand? Jack Tremaine is my dad."

The cop chuckled. "In *your* dreams," he said under his breath.

"In my dreams? Buster, you have no idea. But it's your funeral." I was done talking to this dork. I'd let Dad and his swanky lawyer crucify him.

Twenty minutes or so later through LA traffic, we arrived at the station. I tried threats. I tried seduction. I bawled as the officer hauled me inside. As a last resort, tears usually worked, but not today.

He shifted me in front of a wall marked with lines to show my height.

A woman cop snapped my photo, took my fingerprints, and had me wait in a holding cell. The metal door closed and locked.

I stumbled to a brick wall and reached out to get my bearings. My hand grazed something sticky, and I cringed. *Nasty!* I rubbed my hands hard on the raggedy gray dress and sighed.

The air smelled of spit, puke, and body odor. I tried

to breathe through my mouth, but it made me thirsty. The cage had three rows of wood benches smeared with stains, some already occupied. I searched for a clean, empty place to sit and finally inched in between a brown smudge and a red mark, and stared forward, wide-eyed. I tried to avoid looking at what resembled vomit on the concrete floor to my right.

I heard whispers and giggles to my left. I peered over my shoulder.

A pair of scantily clad women glared back. One had a large Afro, smeared lipstick, and a gold tooth. The other was a petite dishwater blonde with a black eye and sullen expression.

I glanced away, trembling.

In the movies, the one phone call became the saving grace. Tonight, it sucked. Only the stupid limo driver answered. He said he would "see what he could do." What did that even mean? Could this day get any lamer?

I hugged my legs close to my chest and willed myself not to cry anymore. Feasibly, this nightmare would end with me back in my bed. I closed my eyes and exhaled, but when I opened them again, I still lay in the dank cell, and the prostitutes had moved closer.

Chapter Nine

"Cynthia Taylor!" a guard yelled none too soon from outside the white bars. "You made bail. Let's go."

"It's Tremaine, but whatever." I leapt from the bench, relieved. Finally, the joke had ended. I rushed through the sweet door of freedom. Each clang of the bars brought me one step closer.

In the lobby, the cute limo driver waited, arms crossed, and a mean stare that indicated his frustration at having to be there.

Whatever, just do your job. I signed a paper on the clerk's desk, then followed the driver toward the exit.

As he opened the door, I inhaled deep. Outside smelled of eucalyptus and the sea. I smiled, happy to be out. "Where's my father?" I asked, as we crossed to the limo.

Henry held the car door open. "Who's your father?"

No more games. "Um, your employer. Duh."

Henry laughed. "I seriously never get your humor, Cindy. Come on, get in."

Cindy? Too exhausted to fight, I decided to overlook his informal response. I crawled into the back and dropped prone on the seat. I closed my eyes and tried to block out the last six hours. What a traumatic experience. I might need additional therapy after this. First Dad, then the crazy lady, then jail. The absurdity of it all was too much. At some point, I passed out, but I sensed the familiar loop of our driveway and sat up again. The minute the vehicle stopped, I bolted for the stairs, ready for a shower and a twenty-four-hour nap. I climbed two steps.

The dumb driver blocked my path.

"Get out of my way, moron!"

"That's harsh," he said, but not budging.

"Seriously, get out of my way," I repeated, then stepped to my left.

Henry mirrored my movement to his right. "Where are you going?"

"I'm going to bed. What does it look like?" I zigged in the other direction. "That is, if you'd just move out of my way."

He followed again. "You know you can't use the main entrance. Mrs. Tremaine was very clear about that last week. The help always uses the back entrance."

I glared. "Since when does Meredith call the shots around here?"

"Since she signs your paycheck." He seized my arm and tugged me around to the side entrance.

"Paycheck?" I gasped, then tried to shove him off, but he just dug in harder. "What are you talking about, psycho? I don't work for anyone."

"Enough joking around, Cindy. I'm exhausted. Everyone has had it with your attitude. You're lucky to even be here with a job still intact. You have no idea what it took to save your butt today."

I yanked my arm back. "Has everyone gone completely mad? What job do you think I have?"

His gaze rolled down my body.

I glanced down at the maid's uniform and sighed.

"I can explain this."

"Explain?"

I opened my mouth, but nothing came out. What did I say? That my fairy godmother stole my clothes and somehow these just materialized on my body?

"I know you hate your job. But face it, you're just a servant like the rest of us. Stop fighting it. You'll just keep being miserable and making the rest of us miserable." He reached for the door handle, swung it open, and waved for me to enter. "Please try to be good for once. Okay?"

Suddenly, the fairy godwoman's words flooded back through my thoughts. This had to be a joke. I shook my head and stepped back. I pinched the side of my wrist. It stung, but I did it again and again. I had to still be asleep. No way could this be real. I had to be passed out in a bar bathroom somewhere. It wouldn't be the first time. I squinted. Pinched myself again and again until it started to bruise. I didn't care. I wanted to wake up. I needed to wake up. Pinch, pinch, pinch.

Henry snatched my hand. "What are you doing?"

"Trying to get out of this nightmare."

"Come on, crazy." He touched my back and guided me through the open doorway and into the servant's hall.

Though I recognized the space, I hadn't been in this part of the house since age nine or ten. Mainly, because the servants occupied this end, and I had no reason to be here. I considered turning around and running, but right now, I didn't have enough energy to fight. Filthy, tired, and hungry, I'd sleep on the ground if it meant I could close my eyes for a little bit. So, I tailed him down the hallway, though the desire to bolt did not dissipate but increased with the dim florescent lights and narrow plain walls.

He stopped at a door, opened it, and stepped back. "Look, it took major convincing to stop Mrs. Tremaine from firing you last night. You were supposed to serve food at the birthday party, and when she found out you were locked up, she got pretty angry." He shook his head and leaned in. "I begged her, and she gave you one last chance. It's my butt on the line now, so do not screw this up." He pointed to the room and stormed off.

I gaped at the closet-like chamber–dull, gloomy, old-fashioned. Ugly eighties flower artwork decorated the walls. A twin bed, covered in an olive drab blanket and a flat pillow, rested under a small window, and a cheap, press-wood dresser lay next to it. A pair of doors were inset to my left. I walked to them and folded them back to find the tiniest closet ever to exist. "A dog couldn't fit in here." Shaking my head, I faced the room and furrowed my brow. I could easily fit this entire space in my closet upstairs. What was this room anyway? Another prison?

"Welcome back."

I looked up and smiled at the sight of the familiar waif's face. "Ana!"

"It's Eunice." She frowned. "What's wrong with you? Get cleaned up. You're on the clock in fifteen minutes."

"Clock?" I furrowed my brow. "Look, you have to tell someone there's been a mistake."

She rolled her eyes. "Not this again. Henry said you were dreaming about being a debutante again."

My stomach flipped. "But I am—"

"Not," she finished. "Now get ready."

"My clothes are upstairs."

The maid laughed. "Funny." She pointed to another gray dress and white apron hanging on the rack in the small space. "Fifteen minutes." She nodded and walked away.

I flopped back on the mattress, not sure what had just happened. Surely, I had crossed over into some hallucinatory state. Or maybe Freddy lurked close by, ready to knife me. I shut my lids, willing the image to change. Sleep should put things right. Despite the lumpy pillow and mattress, my body relaxed, and I dozed off.

A sudden jolt to my shoulder shook me awake. "What?" I mumbled.

"Cindy!" Eunice snapped.

I moaned and rolled away. "I'm tired."

"Cindy, you're already in trouble. You don't want to do this. Trust me."

"Tea with lime, please."

"Cindy, I'm warning you!"

I peeked and saw the bare and sad surroundings. The nightmare continued. I pushed up and let out a deep breath. "What do you want from me?" Something soft hit my body. I glanced down. The ugly gray uniform lay in my lap.

"Last chance, Cindy. You can get dressed, get into the kitchen, or you can sleep in the street tonight. Your choice." The maid spun on her heel and left.

Would I really end up on the street? The thought of that sent prickles of fear throughout my body. My pulse increased. What if this psycho hallucination was actually real? Not just a horrid nightmare? I gulped. If it was true, then I would be in big trouble. Maybe I should just play along for now, figuring out the truth before dooming myself to a worst fate.

I held the dreadful dress in front of my frame and glanced in a mirror on the wall. A part of me wanted to cry, the other part wanted to punch my way out of here. I didn't understand how I stepped into this place or how to fix it. I needed to contact Dad. He would be so mad at Meredith's actions. This had to be her doing. How hard could it be to pay off the cops and the servants to put on this ridiculous show? "Just wait, witch. Cinderella always destroys her evil stepmonster in the end."

"Be good," a voice echoed. "It's your only way out."

I glanced around. "Who said that?"

Silence.

I peered out the doorway to the empty hallway. Nothing. Obviously, they all believed this nonsense, but if they thought I would work here, they were nuts. First chance, I planned to run upstairs and grab all my stuff and call Dad. But until I could find a phone or computer, I would have to play along. I tucked the dress under my arm and walked down the corridor in search of a shower.

Two doors later, I found a closet with a small toilet, a tiny sink, and a shower no bigger than a coffin. *This can't be it?* A child could not fit in this thing. I stepped back out and walked farther down, but I discovered this floor only had the one bathroom. *How do people live like this?*

I returned, twisted on the water, and squeezed into the minuscule hole. Despite its size, the warm water blanketed every muscle, as the germs washed into the drain below my toes.

Only minutes in, someone pounded on the door.

"I'm in here," I yelled.

"Yes, we know," came Eunice's voice. "You're using up the water. California is in a drought, remember? Ten-minute shower, tops. Now get out. You were expected upstairs a while ago."

Ten-minute showers? That's absurd. I couldn't rinse the conditioner out of my hair in that amount of time. If only this steam could cure the insanity of these people. I shut off the spout, dried my body, and donned the itchy gray uniform. Using the towel, I wiped off the steam from the mirror. The reflection exposed a stranger. The girl in the mirror had dark circles under her eyes, flat, lifeless hair, and no makeup, not to mention a small zit starting to grow on her chin. I refused to know her. "Meredith, you will suffer. Mark my words." I opened the door and watched the steam billow down the hallway.

"Come on," Eunice snapped from the doorway.

I plodded toward her and stepped into the back of the house. For some reason, I remembered the kitchen looking much bigger. Of course, I was a child last time I ventured in here. The industrial-size space had chrome appliances, stainless-steel counter tops, and Spanish tile floors. The smell of bacon and coffee wafted through the air, and my stomach rumbled. It had been a while since I ate, and I felt famished.

Rosa nodded at my arrival.

She had worked in this house since I was a baby and had always been nice, even when I treated her horribly. She could be my way out. "Hey, Rosa. Can you tell these psychotic people to treat me with respect or my father will have their heads?"

The elderly woman tilted her head. "I'm sorry. Who's your father?"

Here we go again. *Not you, too.* "Your boss."

The woman stared at me. Instead of responding, she seized a mop and shoved the pole in my direction. "Clean both the kitchen and the dining room. Once that's done, dust the foyer."

I stepped back from the long stick with crossed arms. "And if I don't?"

Rosa raised an eyebrow and chuckled. "If you don't, *mija*, you'll be living on the street by noon. Your choice."

"The street?" Why did everyone keep threatening the same thing?

"Where else would you go, Cindy? You got no one. Remember?"

Unfortunately, her words rang true. Without my father or his money, I had nothing and no one. I had no friends or support system. What else could I do? My only choice—to work my way out of this nightmare. Just until I saw Dad, and he fixed this. "Can I eat first? I'm starving."

"Once you're done, you may have something to eat." She thrust the mop toward me again.

But this time I took it. "Don't you think I'd work better with a full stomach?"

She clicked her tongue. "Breakfast was served two hours ago. If you wanted to eat first, you should have been up on time. Now, you can wait for our morning snack break like everyone else." Rosa waddled into a walk-in cooler and out of sight.

Whatever. I sighed. The inside of a metal bucket

bubbled on the floor to my right. I dunked the white ball of yarn into the sudsy water and twirled it around. Luckily, as a kid, I sat at the counter and watched the maids work. Usually, because the cook brought me cookies and hot chocolate anytime I visited. Back then, I played nice with "the help." I joked with them and would have even called them "friends." But that was back then, before Mom died, before Meredith invaded, and before I discovered my place in this world. My place? I still knew it. They didn't. Seriously, I don't deserve to be here acting like a servant, performing manual labor.

With each thrust of the mop, more rage seethed in my veins. This was such a ridiculous situation. I blamed my stepmonster—all of this had to be her fault. Somehow, she had convinced the masses to play along with this big joke on me. I had to give her credit for ingenuity, but she would pay. I imagined all sorts of ways to get even, like soaking all of her clothes in fabric dye, removing the toilet seats in the middle of the night, putting baby oil in her shampoo, or sewing all the arms of her garments together. Each prank idea made me smile just a tad more.

I finally finished mopping the floors and approached Rosa. "I'm done."

Rosa handed me an orange, fuzzy thing that resembled a dead cat on a stick.

I stared at it, not sure of its purpose.

"Dust the living areas, feed the dog, then you can have some food."

"Feed the dog?" I pivoted on one hip and crossed my arms. *The dog.* I vaguely remembered one of the stepsisters mentioning it. Now, it was *my* problem.

"Yeah, it's on the back porch. The food is next to her cage."

"I thought you said I could eat after I mopped?"

Rosa tsked and walked away.

No matter how frustrated I felt, the rumbling in my stomach propelled me forward. If it meant I could eat soon, I would do these stupid things. I thought about TV shows where people carried out horrid acts for money or food. I now walked that line. Sleep-deprived, hungry, and destitute, I suffered at my wit's end, ready to do almost anything they asked me to do.

Wasn't that conditioning? Like with soldiers in basic training, they were making me so weak I would do anything. It worked. Right that moment, I figured if it took a little manual labor to get to my immediate goal, I would complete it. I would even kiss the dumb puppy for a pastry. And I assumed the entire staff knew right where I rested—desperate.

They were so cruel. Perhaps they were doing this to get even. They conspired as a group to execute revenge for everything I had done to each of them, which infuriated me even more. But I had no choice, I had to go along with it, for now, but just wait. Revenge would come in a worse package. When this game ended, they would all pay dearly—all of them. I hoped they were eligible for unemployment.

I wiped the fuzzy cat along a bookshelf, the coffee table, a lamp, then turned to the fireplace, and choked on my own spit. I coughed, unable to register what my eyes viewed. The painting over the mantle used to be of Dad positioned behind a chair with Mom and a younger me in her lap. Now, Dad stood with his arms around Meredith and her two girls. I had not just been replaced but erased. Fear crept deep into my core. Could this be more than an elaborate prank?

I lost my appetite. I chucked the duster and sprinted through the living room, then up the stairs, to my old bedroom. I flung open the door and gasped and fell to my knees. A game room—complete with billiards, table tennis, and video consoles—filled the space. I crawled forward and nudged open the closet. It was empty. My bed, my clothes, all my valuables in this world—vanished, poof, gone.

First, the shock made my skin numb, then it was followed by a heavy weight of sadness. I gasped to breathe. I took another step into the foreign space, nauseous.

A cordless phone sat on a corner table under the window. I snatched it up and dialed Dad's office. Surely, he would sort this out.

"May I help you?" his executive assistant answered in her usual smoky voice.

"Hi, Ms. Byrd. Can I talk to my dad?"

"Is this Charlotte or Gabby?"

My mouth dropped open. "Neither. It's Cindy."

"Mr. Tremaine does not have a daughter named Cindy. Nice try, dear. In order to talk to Mr. Tremaine, you must go through your talent agency like everyone else. Have a good day."

The line dropped dead, as my heart plummeted to my stomach. Everything ached. I propped the phone back in its charger and sobbed. Any hope of this being a sick joke or bad nightmare now dissipated. What was this? How could my entire life just disappear because of a stupid birthday wish? Things like that weren't real.

Skittles wandered around the corner. Comforted at

the sight, I reached to pet her.

The tabby's back arched, and she hissed.

I snatched my hand back. "Skittles, it's me."

Without regard for my feelings, she scurried away into the open closet.

No way could Meredith have set that up. Animals knew stuff. They couldn't be coerced like people, right? My eyes pooled with tears at the possibility the fairy godmother was real—that this all might be real.

"What are you doing up here?" Meredith snapped from the open doorway.

The sight of her repulsed me. Furious, I seethed through my teeth, "You! How dare you."

Her thick red eyebrows lifted. "How dare I what? I was ready to fire you last night, but I let you stay because the staff begged me to. God knows why? You're awful to them. Now, if you don't get back downstairs right now and finish your chores, I will fire you for good. I don't care what anyone says. Do I make myself clear?"

The woman's usual friendly disposition had evaporated, her stern voice sounding almost mean. Usually, she came off sickly sweet, but not now. Right this moment, I feared her. She clasped my life in her hands. If I called her bluff, where would I stay? I had no wallet, phone, or anything of value. All of it had disappeared somewhere between here and the jail cell, and the only hope I had left just vanished in a dial tone.

I stumbled past her and down the stairs into the living room. I reached for the discarded duster but didn't use it. Instead, I folded to the carpet and wept. I don't know for how long, but when I stopped, the sun had drifted behind the horizon.

Chapter Ten

"Cindy!" Eunice said from the archway between the living room and entryway. "What are you doing in the dark?"

Before looking at her, I wiped my eyes. I assumed my face had swelled red and puffy. It often got that way when I cried. Hopefully, the unlit room hid this from the maid. "What do you want?"

"Rosa wants you to clean the crystal before dinner."

"Fine. I just need to use the restroom first." I hurried past her, with my face turned away, and darted through the kitchen to the servants' hallway. My stomach cramped, my head throbbed from the intense crying, and my eyes burned from the dried salty tears. I was a complete mess, but I still had one more chore for the night. I entered the small bathroom and avoided glancing in the mirror. I didn't want to know how awful I appeared. Instead, I turned on the faucet and splashed cold water on my face several times, then held a pool of the liquid to my eyes. Slowly, my skin cooled, and my muscles relaxed. Keeping my eyes closed, I fumbled for the towel behind me.

Suddenly, it was in my hand, but someone had placed it there.

I dabbed the scratchy towel to my closed lids and then gazed up. Of course, it would be Henry—always

73

my hero. "Thanks."

"Are you okay?" he asked, with concern in his voice.

"Why wouldn't I be? I'm living the dream," my voice cracked.

He eyed me for a moment, bobbed his head once, and then sauntered down the hall and out the back door.

I drew in a deep breath and exhaled through my lips. I was ready for a ticket out of this nightmare. It was so bizarre, all of it. Maybe I was insane. I rolled the towel back on its rack and shuffled back to the kitchen.

Rosa glanced up from the dough she rolled and glared with pursed lips.

"I was told to clean some crystal?" I asked.

"If you can handle it, they are waiting for you in the family dining room. I need them to shine really well, understand?"

I shrugged. "Okay."

"Okay? It's like talking to a wall. Go, get started. When you're done, you can get yourself something to eat. But we'd rather you ate it in your own quarters tonight."

I shook my head, completely surprised at her blatantly rude behavior. I had known her as the sweet woman who baked me cookies as a kid. Of course, I was the boss's daughter then. This must be who she really was—a nasty, insolent old biddy. When I had my position back, she'd be the first to go. *Bye, bye, Sweetheart. See ya. Hope you like living on food stamps.*

I entered the family dining room and slid into my father's chair at the head of the eight-person table. Instantly, memories slammed back into my conscience.

One night, we had come down for a snack. Dad had tossed a grape at me, and I somehow caught it with my teeth. Dad kept trying to see if he could duplicate the motion. Failure after failure, Mom and I laughed for hours.

In addition, Mom had taught me proper etiquette in this room. "Keep your elbows off the table," she would say. She then pointed out what the different forks meant. Most nights, when we finished our dinner, we remained at the table for hours, telling jokes and stories about our days. It was in that chair on my left, I announced Andy Scott had asked me to go to homecoming. The day Mom died, we had lunched here—potato cheddar soup and egg salad on homemade croissants—her last meal.

I blinked back the tears and reached for the first goblet. The starburst-cut glass with sculpted stems sparkled under the warm light in the room. Though lovely, I didn't even remember owning them.

A cloth rested next to a bin of clear liquid. The aroma of vinegar floated up, pungent and apparent. My best guess—dip the cloth in the vinegar and rub it onto the crystal. So, I did, twenty times. I set the final goblet down, pushed back in the chair, and walked to the kitchen with the tray of glasses. My hands reeked of vinegar. I started to cross to the sink when I heard my name. Rosa and Eunice gossiped about me in the pantry, but I couldn't make out anything else they said. I waited a moment, trying to distinguish their words, but I couldn't. I gave up, flipped on the faucet, and washed my hands.

A pot of something bubbled on the stove, sending a spicy aroma into the air. I lifted the lid and peeked inside. *Chili. Gross.* I didn't really like chili, but my rumbling stomach would tell my taste buds to take a hike and be grateful. I hadn't eaten all day and needed something. Rosa had left a stack of bowls by the pot. I reached for one and dished out a serving. I had just crumbled some crackers on top, when the two women came back in.

"You're not eating in here, right?" Rosa asked, eyes narrowed.

"Rosa, why do you hate me so much?"

She rested her crossed arms over her bosoms. "Who says I hate you? We need to clean up in here, that's all. Now get out so we can do that."

I plunged a spoon into the chili, tucked a bottle of water under my arm, grabbed my bowl with a napkin, and hurried out. I heard them giggle after I left. *Jerks.* I'd get them eventually.

The chili tasted okay. Better than any chili I had eaten before. Or it could be an empty stomach skewed the results. Once I had consumed all of it, I decided to take a walk. I felt cooped up and sad. I needed a break. Outside, the brisk breeze nipped at my skin. I rubbed my arms and skipped down the walkway to the driveway.

Someone leaned under the hood, inside the limo's engine.

"Hey," I said.

Henry peeked over the engine and smiled. "Hey, yourself."

"What are you doing?"

He straightened and wiped his hand on a red cloth. "Checking the fluids."

"Oh," I said, clearly having no idea what fluids he

was talking about. "Well, have fun with that."

"Will do," he said, then returned to his former posture.

I hiked around the mansion, across the lawn, to the hedges below. Once there, I ducked behind one and sat on the stone bench where I had shared my last conversation with Dad. Where he scolded me and prepared to blow my life away with his one birthday wish. I sighed and scanned the fragrant garden. I had been here many times but rarely paid attention to its beauty. Emerald-green trees lined all sides of a stone walkway surrounded by colorful snapdragons, zinnias, and begonias. I knew the flowers' names only because Mom had told me once. She loved anything pretty, and this garden was her baby. Someone had taken care of it over the years. She would have liked that.

A small brook, that emptied into a white, tiered fountain in the center, lapped water. The sound soothed my mind.

A gray robin sporting an orange chest flew over and landed on the tree to my right. It pecked at the trunk, chirping as it did.

Suddenly, colored spotlights flipped on as the last of dusk disappeared.

The bird flew away.

I didn't mind being in the darkness, away from the crazy. I liked it here, peaceful and calm. Here it didn't matter if I had money or not. If people liked me or hated me. I closed my eyes and pictured Mom sitting by my side. Just sitting with me, not talking, but relaxing here for hours.

Mom didn't need to fill space with unnecessary words. "Beauty talked enough," she would say.

I finally understood that sentiment.

"Are you okay out here all alone?"

Startled, I glanced up to see a portly tan man in his late sixties, wearing overalls, a tool belt, and a floppy hat. "What time is it?" I rubbed my eyes, not realizing I must have fallen asleep.

"After eight p.m.," he answered.

"Oh wow, yeah, I should probably go." I stood. "Do I know you?"

The man smiled a crooked smile. "I'm the new gardener, Gus."

"It's nice to meet you, Gus. When did you start?"

"Last week. I'm replacing Jorge."

I nodded, not sure who Jorge was. "Isn't it a little late to garden?"

"Oh, I am just going around, turning on the sprinklers. California law and all, we have to water the garden at night."

"Oh, right." I grinned. "Well, Gus, it was really nice to meet you. I'd better get inside."

The man bent down to a row of begonias, snipped off a pink one, and handed the stem out.

I reached for the flower and smiled. "Thanks. That's very sweet of you."

"Night, Miss." He tipped his hat and stepped back.

"Good night, Gus," I said as I passed him.

For the first time, someone had no former opinion of me. He treated me kindly without reservation. It felt nice. I would remember Gus when I returned to my old life. The rest of them might be fired, but Gus could stay.

Chapter Eleven

"Yes, I'll take another drink," I said, hanging over the bar, slurring to the cute bartender. "And every guy in this place, cute or ugly, is paying for it. Got it?"

"Anything for you, Miss Tremaine." The bartender winked and handed me a bouquet of flowers and a box of chocolates.

I smiled and turned to the room. All gazes were on me. I gulped down the margarita in my hand, then opened my mouth to speak.

A redheaded woman in the front started to laugh, then a dark-haired guy to her left laughed, too. Then, one by one everyone else laughed.

"What are you all laughing at?" I snapped.

They all pointed at my chest. I glanced down. I wore a gray maid's outfit covered in pink bubble gum. I reached to pull the gum off the front, and it stuck to my fingers. I tugged and somehow got it in my hair. The more I pulled, the more it seemed to attach itself like spider webs to my body. I yanked and scraped, and the laughing got louder and louder and—

I opened my eyes, gasping and panting. Where was I? I peered around the dark room. The shapes and outlines were unfamiliar. Fumbling for the lamp on the nightstand, I found the button, clicked it on, and cringed. Even with my eyes open, the nightmare persisted. The tiny maid's quarters still remained and with me in them.

I flopped dramatically onto my back and checked the digital clock. Only five a.m., which was way too early to get up. I switched off the light and tossed to my side, facing the wall. I had just started to drift off again when the overhead light shot on.

"Rise and shine," Eunice sang from the doorway.

I moaned and pulled the scratchy blanket over my head.

"Rosa wants you to peel potatoes. Up and at 'em." She exited down the hall.

But I knew she'd be back if I didn't get up. Besides, today I didn't want to miss breakfast. I wanted to eat. With a roll of my body, I knocked my feet to the floor, and then inched to a stand. The morning air nipped icy and uncomfortable, and goose bumps prickled my skin. *Geez! Don't they believe in a heater down here?* I shuffled down the hall, endured my claustrophobic shower, and donned my pauper's uniform. I could do this. I would do this. Until I didn't have to anymore, then, Lord help all these people who hurt me, because it would get nasty.

I walked into the kitchen.

The staff buzzed around cleaning, prepping, and cooking.

"Just in time for your first chore of the day," the cook said. She placed a pot of potatoes on the counter and slicer next to it.

"Can I at least have a cup of coffee first?"

Rosa glared at me, then nodded. "Go ahead. You might even have a scone, as long as you can work and eat at the same time. We're on a tight schedule today."

I offered a grin that I was pretty sure did not match

the annoyance in my eyes and reached for a mug from the cupboard. As I poured, I watched the sable liquid cascade with steam and bubbles in its wake. The smoky aroma smelled heavenly. I added a splash of hazelnut creamer and sugar, then brought it to my lips. The warmth blanketed my insides. I closed my eyes and imagined sitting on the couch in the den, drinking coffee with Dad. The same sounds and smells I had grown up with still lingered in the house, and for a moment, I was me again.

"I said you could get a cup of coffee, not take a break. Get to the potatoes."

The cook's voice scratched through my reprieve.

A plate of cranberry and orange scones sat on the stove.

I folded a napkin around one and walked it over to the bowl and peeler. Never in my life had I peeled a potato. I had never seen it done either. If I had my phone, I could look it up. But I didn't, so now what? Did I admit this? They had been ruthless since second one. The crew loved to order me around. *Super ridiculous.* No matter what happened, no one wanted to help me. The more I protested, the angrier they got. Of course, so did my snark. I didn't take the insolence well. Rude comments should come from me first. So, I might have been a little bad-mannered, but can anyone blame me? They started it.

But I would try to be nicer today. Hopefully, it would change how they treated me. Since they were hell-bent on making my life miserable, I doubted it. That I was sure of. And the more they did, the more I wanted to fight.

I twirled the kitchen tool in my hand. The peeler

consisted of a plastic handle on one end, and on the other, a metal blade with a slot in the middle. Keeping the potato on the counter, I brought the blade to the spud and swiped down. Nothing happened. I turned it over and tried again. Again, nothing. I flipped it up, over, down, around, only a single sliver of peel came off. I tried for the umpteen time, and the potato catapulted off the counter and rolled across the floor.

Eunice and Rosa peered up from a pile of vegetables, shook their heads, and laughed.

Rosa leaned toward Eunice's ear, whispered, and they both giggled.

"What?" I snapped.

Rosa clicked through her teeth. "You've got to be the worst maid ever."

"Ya think?" I rolled my eyes. Simply put, I wasn't a maid. Obviously, it was not my calling. I bit the side of my cheek, so I didn't cuss her out or tell her off.

"Why are you still here?" Rosa's contempt dripped from her lips.

"Trust me, if I could be anywhere but slumming it with you gals, yeah, I'd be there in a heartbeat."

"I'm over being a charity home for wayward dogs. You want to leave, don't let the door hit your patootie on the way out." She pointed at the exit with her knife.

"Rosa!" Eunice gasped.

"Sorry, but it's true. I don't understand why everyone keeps protecting her. She can't do anything. She's complete trash. Did you see what she did to the crystal yesterday? Full of streaks. I had redo all of them. What's the point of having her here if we have to fix everything she does?"

A struggle boiled within me. Heat radiated through

my face, neck, and limbs. I could have easily retorted. Oh, how I wanted to—so badly—to put the cow in her place. But somewhere deep, very deep, I found the strength to stop myself. I knew any negative action would only cause this to become worse. She would send me packing. I breathed deep, swallowing what pride I had left. "I know I'm not the best servant, but I am trying to change. If you will just have patience, I'll get there eventually."

The woman scowled for a moment, then whispered something to Eunice, and returned to her project without another word.

I attempted, however, without any assistance, to peel that darn potato. Again, and again, the evil vegetable slipped out of my palm and spun onto the floor. At one point, I lifted my hand to chuck the vile gadget across the room, when a strong fist reached for the peeler. I glanced up to see Henry.

He retrieved the lost potato, cupped it in his hand against the counter, then pressed the blade side down against the skin, and a peel slid off.

"How did you do that?" I asked.

"Here." He placed the peeler back in my hand but didn't let go.

His presence sent tingles up my spine. I tried to block them out and pay attention to his demonstration.

He led my other hand to hold the potato and glided my hand alongside to display the action. "You have to hold the potato like this and push hard with the peeler like so."

My heart continued to pound faster in my chest at his touch.

He stepped back and waved. "Now you try."

I stared a moment, then took both in my hands, and mimicked his movements. Amazingly, it worked. The peel slid off, revealing the white meat below. "Oh my gosh. Thank you."

He nodded, crossed to the coffee pot, poured a cup to go, and then sauntered out the back door, as if he had never been there.

Again, Henry to the rescue. I hope being my hero didn't go to his head. Though he was kind and crazy attractive, he was still a *working* man. Still beneath me. Maid or not, I ruled this place—or would. I could not bend to his level. I shook my head to release any delusions that whispered otherwise.

Someday, I would get back to my reality. January first, right? New Year's Eve was only two months away. I could endure anything for that long. I would also find a way to see Dad. I hope that once I talked to him in person, he would remember me, and this would be over. Unfortunately, I didn't remember Dad's cell number. But soon, he'd show up here at the house. I hoped once he saw me, he would remember his *own* daughter, then everything could return to normal.

Next, they had me buff the silver, tidy the living room, and clean the toilets. Apparently, Meredith had guests coming over this afternoon. Finally released, I claimed my lame supper—two pieces of white bread, mashed potatoes, and some unidentifiable pressed meat—and shuffled back to my hovel. I was too hungry not to eat it, but I gagged a little every time I swallowed. Once the hunger subsided, I rejected the rest. I leaned against the wall in my room and sighed. Fresh tears burned my eyes, so I let them fall.

"You want to talk about it?"

I glanced up to see Henry leaning in my doorway. "What do you want?" I wiped my eyes.

He walked in and squatted in front of me. "Just making sure you're okay. You seem to be struggling lately."

"I'm fine," I snapped, more than I meant to.

"Okay then." He held up his hands and moved to go.

"I'm sorry." I touched his elbow. "I'm just stressed. Thanks for checking up on me."

He shrugged, then half-smiled. "Sometimes you can be cool."

"Ouch."

"I'm a very truthful guy."

"I see that."

"But lately, you've been, I don't know, different."

"Is that good or bad?"

He lifted an eyebrow.

I had my answer. I nodded, understanding, *bad*. I toyed with honesty myself. No one, including Henry, had really listened to what I had to say. I prattled on about being someone else, but they saw it as some insane aspiration or spoiled fantasy. Despite the impending response, I chose to try again—to be candid. "I'm different, because my 'truth' is not the same as yours. I think I've somehow stepped into an alternate reality. A real-life nightmare." I pulled my legs to my chest and wrapped my arms around them. "It's the only thing that makes sense. For me, anyway."

"More declarations of dreams?"

"It's not a dream." His attitude annoyed me. Of course, I could understand why he wouldn't believe me. I wouldn't believe me either, but I needed him to. "Can

I tell you how I see this, without you making fun of me or blowing me off?"

He stared a moment, then folded his arms across his chest and shrugged one shoulder. "Sure."

"I am not lying when I say that three days ago, I owned all of this." I spanned my arms as if to encompass the house. "A real-life fairy godmother came to see me, and poof, all of sudden, no one knows the real me anymore."

"A fairy godmother?" His tone wavered on sarcasm.

"You promised not to tease me."

"So, I did."

"And since that's what I remember, it's been super hard. Everyone is treating me like a slave, and my own dad doesn't seem to care or remember me."

Henry crossed the room and sat on the edge of the bed. "No one is treating you like a slave."

I held up a callous on my pinky. "Does this look like the hand of anyone else?"

He drew my finger into his palm to get a better look.

His touch, warm and inviting, drew me to him. Normally, I would recoil, but I didn't, which surprised me.

"You've had that dream before, you know. Where you're rich. We all have. It's what we all want; it just isn't obtainable yet."

"No!" I jerked back my hand and faced him. "See, that's not it. It's not some lofty thing I want or dream about. It's something I had and lost." I pointed around the room, landing on the ugliest watercolor flower painting ever made. "This is the nightmare."

"This is pretty hideous." He laughed. "Who decorated in here?"

I was not amused. "Look, what you're saying is *your* reality. I desire more than anything to wake up, but no amount of pinching seems to work." I held out my purple-and-black wrist, which was bruised with hours of squeezing.

He rolled his hand under my bruised limb. "You're a mess."

"You think?"

He smiled.

His thumb lightly grazed the base of my hand, sending butterflies through my body. "Do you like me?" I asked, surprising myself that I spoke.

He let go of my arm and didn't respond.

"It's fine. I get it. I'm not easy to like." I sighed. "I just wonder why you keep helping me if you loathe me like the rest of them."

"You can be a bit harsh sometimes, but I'm pretty convinced, somewhere deep inside you, there's something worth liking."

We locked gazes, and for a second, a thick tension formed between us, but then, we both laughed.

"Fair enough." I glanced down at my shoe and noticed a small rip in the top seam between the cloth and the rubber. "Great. Now my one and only pair of shoes is torn."

"I'll see if I can find some duct tape or something."

I giggled. "Yes, because duct tape fixes everything."

"Exactly." He walked back to the door. "Night."

I smiled. "Night."

He closed the door.

I laid back and dropped my stare to the scratchy green blanket beneath my leg. How I wished I would wake up. I flipped off the light. Shadows cast on the walls from perimeter lights coming through the small window above my bed. I watched them dance, and it took me back. I visualized lying on Mom's bed when I was five. We spent hours there, imagining animals, monsters, cars, angels... *Man, I miss her.* Alone, in the dark, the infuriating emotions inundated me again. Depressed, I rolled over and moaned into my pillow. First, I lost my mother, then all my friends, now my dad, and all my worldly possessions. I had nothing left but a life of servitude. I closed my eyes and wept into the folds of cotton.

The fairy godmother said something about my "being good" would help me get everything back. But how did I do that? Be good. What did that even mean? Did it mean being nice to people? I cringed a little. Did it mean helping the poor, feeding the homeless, or donating a kidney? I gave to the less fortunate already. I didn't fully get what the fairy godmother wanted. Maybe I should have asked Henry. He seemed like a good person. Always coming to my rescue, even when I didn't want or ask for it. My stomach flipped as he drifted through my thoughts.

Perhaps being his friend wouldn't be so bad. I could use a friend about now. Normally, with money and power, friendship came at a price, but now, without both, I needed the support. It wasn't like he wanted anything from me or that I had any of value to give him.

Beyond Henry, what did "good" look like? What good person did I know? A sweet girl from high school flashed in my mind. Her name was Sheila. No, wait, Shelly? Or was it Stella? I frowned. *Who cares? Some "S" name. Geez.* I rolled back onto my back, hitting the bed with my arms. *Focus.* So, what made her good? To start with, she used to say "please" and "thank you" all the time. Completely hilarious, they voted her most likely to be a nun. A perfect brownnoser—teachers loved her, and, of course, I hated her. But she was a decent human being.

Surely, the fairy godmother wanted an "S" girl. Maybe that's what I needed to be, more like Ms. S. Tomorrow, I would attempt the impossible and try to be a perfect angel. Actually, be nice to people, say "please" and "thank you," and smile and encourage. I might even attempt to make friends. At the thought, I winced and threw up in my mouth a little. But inside, I knew I had this. In truth, I needed this to take steps to crawl out of this gaping hole before it swallowed me permanently. And maybe, just maybe, succeed in having this psycho pixie come back, flick her wand to get me the heck out of the dungeon, and back to my real life.

Chapter Twelve

The insufferable alarm blasted at 6:00 a.m. I leapt out of bed, showered, dressed, and then waited on the edge of the mattress.

At 7:00 a.m. sharp, Eunice flung open my door, and her mouth dropped ajar.

I was ready for her to "rise and shine" me, but instead, she closed her mouth and crossed her arms, her eyebrows dipping. "You're up?"

"Ready to serve." I grinned a bit too wide.

"Um...great." She glowered a moment longer, then waved for me to follow her to the kitchen. "Breakfast is ready, and whatever cook made, it smells amazing. Once we're finished eating, we will clean up after Meredith's dinner party from last night."

The name of my stepmonster made me twitch. While I lived in squalor, Meredith now hosted parties in *my* childhood home, in *my* dining room, with *my* inheritance. "Absurd," I hissed under my breath.

Eunice turned back. "What's that?"

"Awesome."

Eunice shook her head, her dishwater-blonde ponytail swinging side to side.

I would do this good thing and bite my true feelings. I wanted to say, *Why should we have to clean up after her?* but instead, I asked inside, *What would Ms. S do?* I squared my shoulders. I had to be Ms. S. It was why I got up early this morning, ready to go. I might have had a slow start, but I had this.

After a quick breakfast of cinnamon rolls and coffee, we ventured into the formal banquet area. When I was growing up, we hardly ever used this space. Dad preferred to eat in the family dining room. He said it was cozier. I agreed, but I still admired the beauty of this room. Tall ceilings with gold-leaf molding and an eight-light crystal chandelier, a long, cherry wood table and champagne, covered chairs sat on a burgundy Persian carpet. The chandelier lit the room in soft orange hues. The room could be a little dreary. I always said it needed windows. Dad said he didn't see the value of cutting into the wood paneling on the outside wall. My counter argument was the rest of the house screamed twenty-first century, while this one was stuck in 1972. We had a good laugh, but he always won—his money, his house, his rules.

Now, rows of discarded cloth napkins, dirty glasses stained with lipstick, and crumbs lined a long white tablecloth.

Eunice pointed toward a gray tub a few feet away.

My new role was *busser?* The thought of cleaning after others grossed me out. Touching the leftover dishes that actually came in contact with someone's mouth was nasty. Maybe being exposed to COVID-19 made me a germaphobe, but who wasn't these days? Using only my thumb and forefinger, I pinched the glass stem and set it into the tub. I did this over and over, trying not to clank them as I laid them into the bin.

Eunice hummed nearby.

Her resting expression was always smiling and

content. How could anyone be so happy all the time? My default setting was miserable. Possibly some poor soul actually liked her? What else could make someone cheerful twenty-four-seven? Love, I suppose. Though, how would I know? I had never experienced anything close to love, and I didn't intend to. Men were for sport. Anything more would end in eventual pain. This I was sure of. I had had enough pain and loss in my life, so I avoided any potential threat at all costs. "Can I ask you a question?"

She withdrew an earplug from an ear. "Yeah?"

"Why are you so happy all the time?"

The waif puckered her lips for a second before responding. "Life is what you make of it, Cindy. You decide every day whether you are going to be happy or sad, angry or calm. I choose joy." She winked, then stuck her pod back in her ear.

As I reflected on my life, I considered happiness. Since Mom died, I conscientiously decided to be irritated with the world and to blow off anyone close to me. Eunice spoke the truth. I chose misery. It was just easier that way. I carried the full bucket back into the kitchen and set it in the sink.

The cook pointed toward the dishwasher and walked back to a cutting board to cut up a chicken.

I sighed and opened the door to the enormous machine. Carefully, I deposited one of the flutes inside the top rack.

"No, dumb girl. You can't put those glasses in there," Rosa said behind me. "Just the coffee mugs and bread plates. You will need to wash the glasses by hand."

Inhale, exhale. It's my choice to decide it's okay.

I'm okay. Don't get angry. Inhale. Exhale. No matter what anyone said, I would just nod and smile. So, I did. I spun back to the sink and flipped on the water. Of course, the cook had to come demonstrate how to wash a wine glass by hand. But once she did, I completed the task without a hitch. "Thank you," I managed to squeak out. "I finished the dishes."

"Sweep the floors," Rosa ordered.

I nodded and smiled.

"Dust the rooms."

I nodded and smiled.

"Empty the trash."

Yep, a nod and smile. It was a tad crazy, but somehow, it worked.

The staff seemed to let up some, too.

By dinnertime, Rosa returned my nod and smile.

I folded and hung my apron by the back door and shoved the revolving door.

"Ouch!" a male yelled.

I stepped back, with eyes wide and heart pounding.

Henry peeked around with hands cupped over his nose.

"Oh, my gosh. I am so sorry. Are you okay?"

He laughed and dropped his hands. His face was fine, as always. "Just joking."

I swatted his bicep. "Not funny."

He held up a thumb and finger an inch apart. "A little funny?"

I shook my head, and then returned his smile.

"Are you done for the day?" he asked.

"Yeah. You?"

"Yep. I came to see if you'd want to go grab a coffee?"

I glanced a few feet away.

Rosa and Eunice sat at the counter, eating a chicken casserole, deep in conversation.

"Are we allowed to leave?" I whispered.

He laughed and leaned to mimic my whisper. "We're not prisoners here. If we're off the clock, we can do whatever we want."

Best news ever. "Cool, yeah. Let's go. I haven't seen the real world in over a week. Give me a second to change."

"I'll meet you at the entrance."

I slid past him and started walking to my room, then stopped at the realization that the only clothes I owned was this awful gray uniform. I swallowed my pride and walked back to the kitchen. "Eunice?"

Her gaze met mine. "Yeah?"

"Um, any chance I could borrow something of yours to wear?"

She set her fork down and slid out from the stool. Without a word, she walked past me and out the kitchen door. A moment later, she placed a pair of folded black yoga pants and a red tee in my arms. "I don't think you'd fit my jeans, but you could probably squeeze into these, and the shirt was the former maid's. It's too big on me, anyway."

"Thank you," I said more humbly than I can remember speaking, especially since she kind of implied I was *fat*. I decided to let it go this time; after all, it was nice of her to give me clothes.

She returned to her casserole.

If anyone had a reason to hate me, that woman did. I acted like a jerk on purpose, but she showed me kindness. Of course, she didn't remember I had treated her like a jerk before all this, but I knew. Somehow, deep in the recesses of my spider-webbed heart, her kindness touched me.

I returned to my room and slid my legs into the pants. They were a tad tight, but they worked. The T-shirt fit well but was hardly stylish. It didn't matter. I'd do anything to be out of that ugly gray dress for a while. I ran a hand through my hair, pinched my cheeks, then met Henry at the front.

"Scored some clothes, did you?" He grinned.

"Yes. Though, don't judge me."

"Judge you? Why would I?"

"They aren't my usual style."

"Sounds like you're the only one judging."

I laughed. "I guess so."

He opened the passenger side of a small truck and stepped back.

I slid in and grinned. For a brief second, I felt like a normal girl—no cleaning and scrubbing or sitting in the servants' quarters sulking. Just a girl on her way to have coffee with a cute guy. I wanted to have fun and feel alive again. I decided I would attempt to follow Eunice's advice and choose joy from now on. A foreign concept I hoped I could pull off. I'd sure try.

The ride to the coffee shop caught me by surprise. A warm peace settled in my chest as Henry told me story after story. In truth, I didn't usually listen to other people's stories. I mostly tuned them out and waited until I could share my own. Or I would jump in to cut them off because I didn't care—or wanted to care. But right now, I didn't have much to say or share anyway, and it seemed cool to just listen for a change. "Do you have any other funny stories?"

He pressed his lips together and dipped his two eyebrows.

I waited.

"Yeah, one. I was waiting for this mechanic friend of mine to check my tires. It was a really nice day, so I was standing outside checking my phone, when he comes out with this woman." He glanced at me and then continued, "She walks the mechanic to this white muscle car, and the guy is like, 'Oh, nice ride.' And the woman is like, 'Yeah, I know, right?' So, the mechanic checks the pressure of all the tires, then turns to the lady, asking, 'Can you open it, so I can check the mileage?' " Henry laughed, obviously struggling to finish. "So, she clicks the remote, and a car door opens three stalls over."

"No way?" I giggled. "It wasn't her car?"

Henry shook his head, laughing. "No."

"Did she even own a muscle car?"

"Yeah, which makes it even funnier, because when the mechanic gets to her car, he says, 'Oh, I see we've downgraded.' "

"Ooh, that's so lame," I groaned. "The poor girl."

"Yeah, we laughed about that for a week." He rolled the truck against the curb, turned off the engine, and came around to let me out.

I couldn't believe how relaxed I felt.

When we got to the coffee shop door, he opened it for me.

It was the first time someone had served me in over a week. As I passed by, I smiled.

He returned the smile.

Inside, soft jazz played in the background. Post-millennials and hipsters lounged around the room on fuzzy high-backed chairs, typing, talking, or texting.

We weaved through the small crowd to the counter.

A woman in short dreads entered from the back and approached us. "What can I get you two?"

"She'll have a hazelnut-vanilla coffee with a shot of espresso, half-and-half, and a Splenda?" Henry winked.

How did he know my drink? "So, we've done this before?"

A coy smile pinched at his lips. "Except I'm usually in line behind you, and you refuse to sit with me."

Now that sounded more like something I would do.

"I'll have a dirty chai latte," he said.

"Gross," I whispered.

He tilted his head sideways. "What? You don't like that?"

"No." I laughed. "I had it once. Tea and espresso do not go together. One sip, and I wanted to puke."

"Nice."

"You asked."

"Anything to eat?" the lady asked.

The food at the house never tasted great. I ogled the pastries one-by-one. My mouth watered at the sight of sticky cinnamon buns swathed in candied pecans and caramel. I let my gaze drift over the shelves filled with lemon cupcakes piled high with yellow buttercream frosting and sprinkles, raspberry scones dripping in sweet glaze, and blueberry muffins laced with powdered sugar and crumbles. *How did one decide?* I pointed toward a flaky puff pastry smothered in dark black cherries and drizzled in cream cheese frosting.

"We'll take that, and I'll have a bear claw," he

said.

Balancing plated pastries and mugged drinks, we crossed to a couple of tall stools at a corner café table.

I tried to pace myself with the dessert, but it tasted so good. Each bite of the buttered sugary goodness melted in my mouth. I skimmed a finger over the dropped crumbs and licked my finger.

"If it's that good, I can get you another one," Henry said, with an amused smile.

I nudged the empty plate away. "Sorry, I've just been so hungry for yummy food."

We sat in silence for a few minutes. I didn't know what to say, so I waited. Usually, I could small talk, but for some reason, I didn't feel like talking about anything unimportant. I think the reality of everything had finally started to take its toll. Out of nowhere, a sadness washed over me.

He leaned forward. "So, tell me what has been going on. Are the nightmares just becoming too real?" Henry took a sip of his coffee and then said over the brim, "It might be time to go see someone."

"See someone?" I raised an eyebrow. "You mean like a shrink?"

He nodded.

"I'm not crazy."

His stare linked with mine.

His gaze appeared to hold genuine concern. Could this stranger actually care about me? Why would he? He barely knew me. But it didn't seem to be mean-spirited suggestion. Simply put, he couldn't understand. How could he? My truth had a supernatural, unrealistic bent. What would it take for this man to believe me? That somehow, I had stepped into some alternative universe, and I wasn't really the maid he thought I was. I had tried to convince him before and obviously had failed miserably. Explaining would only make him insist even more on a psychologist. I didn't know what to say, and it exhausted me to think about it. So, without responding, I reached for a napkin and wiped my hands instead.

He placed his elbows on the round table and leaned forward. "Look, you just seem super unhappy. I hate when people are sad. It makes me sad, you know?"

"Would you consider me a friend?"

He looked down at the table without a word.

"So, we're not?" I nodded. Of course. Not even in this mixed-up universe did I have anyone in my life. Why would I? What did the fairy godmother call me? Wretched? The truth hurt. I knew it. The biggest mystery was why all of a sudden, I cared. I never cared before, and there was a reason for that. Caring stung. Caring cost. Caring could destroy me.

"Well, to be fair, this is the first time we've ever really hung out or talked without you insulting me." He lifted his mug and sipped, a glint of a smile in his eyes as he peered over the rim.

"Sorry about that." I don't know if I meant it because I never apologized to anyone ever. Out of nowhere, a powerful emotion of sorrow clutched my chest. My throat closed as my eyes welled with tears. I needed to roll the feelings away before they controlled me. If I didn't, I would burst out sobbing right then and there.

He set his cup down and reached out to my shoulder with his free hand. "Are you okay? Did I hurt your feelings?"

Did he? No, not really. "I just feel so alone."

"Not to sound callous," he said, withdrawing his hand, "but I thought you liked it that way."

Sure, in the past I had told myself that lie. Pushing people away seemed safer, but in all honesty, who really liked being alone? "I might pretend, but it's not pleasant."

"Yeah, I get that."

I wrapped my hands around the warm mug, unsure what to say next. I needed so much for this person to understand how I felt. I wanted an ally. As insane as it might have been, for the first time in years, I desired a friend.

"I'm a pretty good listener. You can share anything. I promise not to judge," he said.

I licked my lips, hoping for the right words. "Promise that you won't call me psycho or insist that I need to see a shrink again?"

"Okay, I promise."

I set my cup down and shifted forward, so he could hear me as I lowered my voice. "Nightmare or not, my reality is somehow skewed. For you, this has been going on forever. For me, it has only been a week. I remember living not as a servant, but as the one who orders servants around."

He bristled.

Did I dare go on? I had to. "I'm confused. The other world—the one you say is a recurring nightmare—that's the one that's real to me. This—" I spun a finger around in a circle. "This feels off. Not normal. I can't explain it. I know I've told you this over and over, but this isn't my real life. I wish I could somehow convince you...." I trailed off, not sure how

100

to finish.

"Did you hit your head?"

Did I? I thought back to the bar parking lot when that drunk idiot pushed me. No, I don't think so. I would remember that. Or would I? Nothing made sense. "Who knows, but something is not right. I feel it. I know it."

"I'll admit, you're a little more pleasant than usual." He winked.

I playfully kicked his shoe with mine. "Jerk!"

"Now, there's the Cindy we all know and love." He smiled. "Look, I'll try to help you figure it out, okay?"

"Really? You'd help me, even though I've not been very nice?"

He pursed his lips together, then slowly allowed them to melt into a grin. "Yeah, sure. Damsel in distress, why not?"

"Thank you, Henry." I downed the rest of my coffee, excited that I might actually be able to trust someone. I hoped he could help me get back to my old life. But if he did, would it be the same?

Chapter Thirteen

Around a year ago

I turned a page of my latest fashion magazine in an attempt to block out the chaos in the house. My stepsisters couldn't seem to move their stuff in quietly. For two hours, they had dragged, dropped, and delivered their boxes with a thunderous annoyance. And they sang show tunes, continuously giggled, and made the obscenest sounds that I refuse to even try to define.

Who makes that much noise, anyway?

Luckily, they had to share the other suite with each other, and I got to keep my own room to myself. It was a good thing, too. If I heard Dad say anything different, I would have unleashed a bratty fit like no other. I assume some otherworldly wisdom must have guided the decision. However, Dad had hinted about finding a bigger house. As if a mansion with four suites, a half-dozen servants' quarters, several guest rooms, a formal dining room, a full library, a den, a large living room, a media room, a commercial-size kitchen, a pool with a pool house, and five acres of garden in Beverly Hills was not enough for a family of four.

Besides, Mom had lived here. She helped me decorate my bedroom—picked out this gray wool carpet, painted the champagne walls, and hung the ivory sheer drapes. Irreplaceable memories. This room meant a lot. Lord help Meredith if she ever tried to get rid of any of these.

The two girls stumbled down the hallway and landed in my doorway, giggling and shoving each other. Both were just a few years younger than me, but maturity-wise, it seemed more like five. "What?" I snapped.

Charlotte revealed her metal-covered teeth in a hideous grin. "We were thinking about going into town to buy some stuff to decorate our new room. We wanted to know if you want to come tag along?"

"Now that we're sisters, it would be great to get to know you more," Gabby added.

"No, I'm good," I said, not looking up from the magazine.

Gabby dared to step forward. "I know this is hard on you, Cindy, but we really want to become a family. It would help if we—"

"You want to know what would really help, Gabby?" I peered from one sister to the other. "Do you, Charlotte?"

The two girls nodded enthusiastically.

"Bring me a cup of tea and some aspirin. I have a terrible headache."

They glanced at each other, then scrambled out of the room.

The idea flowed through my head. Maybe I could use them to serve me and make them my personal slaves. If they cleaned for me and brought me things, then it wouldn't be so bad to have stepsisters. A sardonic grin spread across my face. Yes, I could make it worth it. This family would never know what hit them.

****

Present Day

Gabby and Charlotte laughed and hung onto each other as they stumbled down the steps and out the front door.

They giggled more than anyone I had ever met. I shook my head and stepped on the button on the top of the vacuum. The machine purred to life. As my thoughts drifted, my vison blurred. I moved back and forth, probably longer on one spot than necessary. I needed to figure out my options. How could I get out of this horrible situation? I usually excelled at schemes—well, usually, conniving deep, dark, and devious plans. I knew how to do evil well. Stir up trouble. Be awful. I was the villain, not the princess, as my fairy godmother realized all too well. Malicious deeds I could accomplish easily.

But fixing things by being good—yeah, I had nothing. Not to mention, any plan, without any kind of resources or money, seemed impossible. Worse, I no longer had my father's ear. Dear old Dad was the reason most of my scheming had worked. For better or worse, he backed me. And if my plans didn't succeed, he bailed me out. Without him, this ship just might sink without a life raft. I heard a voice squeak through my thoughts. I peered up.

Eunice glared only a few feet away with arms crossed.

I turned off the machine. "Sorry. I couldn't hear you. What did you say?"

"I said, I think that spot is clean."

I blinked, then nodded. "Right, sorry. Daydreaming, I guess." I turned the vacuum back on, then glided it across the cream carpet, watching the long wool fibers flatten, then pop back up. Out of all the chores Rosa had asked me to do, I liked this one the best. The soft purr and lack of brain power needed made the task tranquil, almost therapeutic. *That is if I remember to move.*

Eunice walked in front of the vacuum and blocked my path.

I shut it off again. "What's up?"

She eyed me with a narrow stare. "In all of the years I've known you, you have never apologized to me for anything. Usually, there's some awful retort. What's going on with you lately?"

That's because you were just a maid, and I was your boss. I shrugged. "I am not sure, to be honest. Things are just off somehow. But I thought you'd wanted me to be nicer."

"I'm not complaining, I'm just wondering what you're up to."

I held up my palms in mock surrender. "Nothing. Just trying to be a better human, that's all." Her expression remained blank, her stare focusing on me for an uncomfortable amount of time. I opened my mouth to break the awkward silence.

But she spoke first. "The cook just made a fresh pot of coffee and maple nut scones. When you finish vacuuming, you should come get some."

Now *she* acted nice. Interesting how one seemed to precede the other. "Thanks. That sounds great."

Eunice bobbed her head once, then walked back to the kitchen.

Scones? The mere word made my stomach rumble. Now, I had a reason to hurry. No more daydreaming. I moved the vacuum back and forth, back and forth, hitting every corner at record speed. I shut it off, returned it to the closet, and rushed toward the kitchen. Right before I pushed the door open, I heard my name. I paused and peeked through the French slats to eavesdrop.

Eunice toyed with the corner of a scone. "There's something weird about her. I don't trust her. She could be up to something."

"Yeah, like the bubble incident," Rosa said.

"Or the time she had Meredith blame me for the scratches in the hall," Eunice said.

"Oh, yeah, that was bad."

"There's no way she is being nice to be nice. I mean, is that even possible? A monster does not change her spots. Right?"

Not sure that is how that saying goes.

Rosa said something I couldn't make out.

Eunice nodded.

"I agree with you. I don't trust her either. What we need to do is keep an eye on her. Period."

Eunice slid from the stool, crossed to the coffeepot, and refilled her cup. "You know me, I'll be friends with almost anyone. But her? She's vicious. I've tried a few times, but, well, you know how that ended. The nicer I am, the more the knife goes in."

Rosa shook her head, tsking with her tongue. "They should have fired her forever ago, but that mysterious family connection always stops them."

Harsh! I wasn't sure how to feel. Hurt? Angry?

"Yeah, what is that, anyway?" Eunice shook a

packet of sweetener, ripped it open, and let the granules rain into her cup.

"Nobody really knows for sure. Just that Mr. Tremaine came in here one day to speak to the staff. He said that Cindy was somehow family, and we needed to give her room and board in exchange for work. He said that Meredith wasn't to know about that connection, but that we were all to fight for her. Our jobs depended on it."

My stomach somersaulted. *Family? So, he still thinks I'm family.* That made me feel a little better.

"Where was I?" Eunice asked.

"I think at the doctors," Rosa said.

"Well, why didn't you tell me that earlier? You just told me and Henry to fight to keep her, but not why. I never understood it. That would have helped some."

"Sorry, I probably should have told you before now," Rosa said.

"What do you suppose the connection is? Some love child or something?"

Rosa shrugged. "Beats me. Whatever it is, I wish it didn't matter to him."

"Yeah."

The two sat in silence for a moment, and then changed the subject of their gossip to someone I had never heard of.

I pushed through the doors and crossed to the coffeepot. A row of white porcelain mugs hung on hooks by the maker. I reached for one and poured myself a cup. I sensed their gazes on my back. No way would I let this get to me. I never cared what people thought of me before. Why start now? Besides, I had enough grief. I didn't need these catty women to add to it. I sat on one of the wooden stools at the other end and proceeded to lighten my coffee with a few teaspoons of half-and-half and a sweetener.

Okay, I couldn't lie to myself anymore. Their words stung. No one expected much of me, but perhaps I could prove them all wrong with some sort of backwards justice. I glanced up and encountered Rosa's stare.

"Cindy, what's going on with you, really?" Rosa spat.

No sugarcoating it. These women played direct.

I respected that to some degree. I circled my spoon in my coffee, then placed it down on the marble countertop. "Before I answer your question, can you tell me what you remember about me? Before I went to jail?"

The two exchanged glances but said nothing.

I needed an in. Some way to get these women to tell me what I wanted to know, without them thinking I was a lunatic. "You want to know what was different about me. Sure, I'll tell you."

The women leaned in.

I prepared to do my best storytelling. "Something happened to me the night I was in the jail cell that erased some of my memories. I know you can tell things are off with me—" I took a deep, dramatic pause, as if I was about to reveal some major truth, "I lost part of my past that night. My memory is almost completely wiped—gone. I know you don't like me much, but please help me fill in the gaps. How did I act before going to jail?"

Eunice laughed, then covered her mouth with a hand. "Rosa?"

"Honestly, you were mean. You thought you were above all this." Rosa glanced around the room, twirling a finger in a circle. "As if an orphaned maid had any right to say she was better than us."

I dropped my gaze to my coffee cup. I took a deep breath to calm my anger because I needed them to continue, but the word "orphan" disturbed me. I wasn't an orphan. Just because Dad didn't remember me didn't mean anything. My father still lived. Besides, I was *not* a maid, and I had every right to act the way I wanted. They just didn't know who I was, that's all. I hoped understanding would help me figure a way out of this mess. "What else?"

"You would say things like, 'Someday I'll be all of your bosses, and you'll serve me,' " Rosa said.

They both laughed.

"Sometimes you would demand I bring you tea, even though I am your equal," Eunice added.

So, she remembered that, just in a different context. *Interesting.* "And you didn't fire me?"

"We don't have the authority to fire you, dear, but if we did, you would have been gone a long time ago," Rosa sneered.

I took a sip of my coffee—rich and smooth. I waited a moment before asking the ultimate question. "So, who keeps me here? Who protects me?"

The women once again exchanged glances.

"Mr. Tremaine asked us to protect you. He said that you were related to someone in his family who died and that we should take pity on you," Rosa said.

If Dad knew me, then I had a slight pinch of hope. "Did he say what family member?"

Rosa shook her head. "No, we never questioned it.

He's the boss, you know. We just follow orders."

"But Meredith wants to fire me," I said.

Rosa picked up a crumb from her plate and plopped it into her mouth. "She never understood why her husband would want to hire someone so rude, but he secretly asked us to keep you as a favor. He said that no matter what, we were to fight to keep you, without Meredith knowing why."

I shifted from one foot to the other. I feared asking, but I had to. "Is this his first marriage?"

They shook their heads together.

"He had another wife and child, but both died."

The coffee traveled down my throat wrong, and I started to cough. My eyes watered and burned.

Rosa rushed to get me a cup of water.

Eunice patted my back.

After a few sips of water and deep breaths, I managed to get it under control. In their minds, his daughter had died. The debutante who held Daddy's heart no longer existed. It had finally happened. Meredith and her children had completely replaced me. But who was I to him? How did he think I fit into this family? It didn't make sense. Only the voodoo magic of an evil fairy godmother could cause such an alternative universe to exist.

Could I call her? I needed to understand. I wanted to know more. "I'll be back. I need a personal break."

"As long as you're back in ten. I need you to change the sheets in the bottom floor guest room," Rosa said.

"Will do." I snatched a scone from the plate and a napkin and darted through the kitchen to the back entrance into the dark and empty corridor. My canvas shoes squeaked on the tile, as I sprinted down the servants' hallway to my room. I shut the door and propped on the side of my bed. I didn't know if this would work, and she would come. I hoped, but I didn't know for sure. "Oh, fairy godmother? It's me, the wretched Cynthia Tremaine." My voice echoed in the quiet space. "If you can hear me, would you please come talk to me? I'm ready to listen. I promise. Please."

Nothing.

"I know I've been awful. I am super aware that I need to change. That I have changed. I've learned my lesson. Please. Don't ignore me. I really need to speak to you."

Zero response. *Lame.*

"Some fairy godmother you are." Wasn't her mission to make my life better and come help when I fall to my lowest place? *Kind of there now.* "Look, I don't know what I can do. Who does my father think I am?"

Zilch.

I dropped back to the mattress with a huge sigh. Pointless. I closed my eyes, wishing to just sleep. Sleeping seemed to be the only time I didn't feel terrible. For a moment, my brain recalled fun times—the parties, the jewelry, the clothes. "Oh, how I miss the clothes," I said, out loud.

"Clothes really do not make the woman," came the melodic tone of my fairy godmother.

I shot to my feet and smiled. "You came!"

The woman wore a flowing white caftan, and her salt-and-pepper hair hung in hundreds of waist-length braids. As always, her makeup appeared flawless and glowing. "So, you're ready to be good then?"

"Yes, yes, yes." Was it that simple? Would she zap me back now?

My fairy godmother shook her head. "No, it's not that simple, Cindy. You haven't proven anything yet."

I grunted. "I've been playing nice. I've been mopping, scrubbing toilets, and look—" I held up my left hand. "Callouses and broken nails. Total blue-collar hands. Gross, right? But I did it with a good attitude."

"Cindy, if I put you back in your life right now, you'll end up the same way. Maybe if you're nice for a week or two, if we're lucky, but then you'd go back to pushing people around and acting superior. It would not be long before your dad lost it."

The mention of my father stabbed a bit. I hated that I had hurt him. If there was anything I wanted to change, it started there. "I am sorry about my dad. I'm sorry I hurt him. I want to fix that."

"As I said before, Cindy, you have until New Year's Eve at midnight. If you have genuinely changed by that deadline, then you'll get your life back. If not, this will be your life forever, and your protection will be gone. You will not be allowed to stay here any longer." She rotated a finger in a circle, and then glared at me. "You will have to leave and find work somewhere else."

I gawked, open-mouthed. "I cannot live like this forever. I miss my life. I miss my dad."

She nodded. "I understand. That's why the choice is yours to make. Fight for him. Now, if you'll excuse me, I have other clients to attend to."

I stepped forward. "Wait! I have another question."

She titled her head sideways, her expression tight.

Would she deny me the question? "Fine. What?"

"Who does my dad think I am?"

A slow grin slipped across the woman's face. "He thinks you are his sister's illegitimate child. An embarrassment to the family who your dad wishes to keep a secret."

"What? That doesn't make sense. My aunt never had kids."

The woman laughed. "I know, but I had to have a reason for them not to fire you. Because I knew you'd be horrid, and that would be a hard ask. So, I blinded the truth and gave them a new reality."

"And that's what you came up with? A love child?" My skin crawled.

She smirked.

Man, she annoyed me. "One more question?"

"Because I'm in a generous mood, sure, fine. What?"

I cleared my throat, almost afraid to ask. "On January first, if I have been good, will anyone here remember me?"

She pinched her lips together, then approached me with a soft frown. "I'm afraid not, dear. You can't have both worlds."

"That's awful."

"I know, and I'm sorry." She waved and vanished, but not before the final words, "Be good, Cindy. Be good."

Be good? How did one do that exactly? I sighed. *I'd better figure it out—or else.*

Chapter Fourteen

On Sundays, the staff took the day off, so I slept until noon. When I finally woke, my muscles ached and my head pounded. I would have slept for another few hours, but the burning in my stomach said I required food more than sleep. I wandered into the kitchen, barefoot and dressed in the clothes I had borrowed from Eunice. Silence encased the house, and I wondered if anyone remained. That would be fine by me—a day alone.

I rummaged through the refrigerator and cabinets in search of anything edible. Back when I influenced the shopping of this household, the cupboards exploded with sugary cereals, chocolate-frosted donuts, toaster pastries, and peach instant oatmeal. Now, it seemed, Meredith's "bunny food" had taken over. Whole grain cereal, fiber bars, bran muffins, and flax oatmeal—how could anyone live like that? I'd be on the toilet night and day. I smiled at the thought, then frowned again. None of the choices sounded good, and the sad reality was I had no idea how to cook. I reached into the fridge and grabbed a piece of soy cheese. Grimacing, I bit into it, just as the door behind me banged closed. I spun around, the slice of bogus cheddar still hanging between my teeth.

Henry smiled. "Did I catch a mouse stealing some cheese?"

I swallowed and palmed the rest. "If you can call it that. Honestly, I'm starving and have no idea what to eat. It's all nutritious and disgusting—I don't even think you can truly call it food. More like cardboard in fancy packaging."

Henry laughed.

I liked his laugh, friendly and deep, but not guttural; it always put me at ease.

"Rosa usually leaves some casseroles in the back of the fridge for the staff to eat."

The smell of aftershave lingered behind him as he crossed by me.

He opened the fridge door, squatted, pushed a few jars out of the way, then produced a rectangular glass dish covered in foil. "Here we go." He set it on the counter and winked. "This is the good stuff." He lifted the foil.

I peered at what looked like creamy, light-green mush under melted cheese. My nostrils flared in slight disgust. "What is it?"

He laughed. "It might not look great, but I promise, it tastes wonderful."

"But what *is* it?"

"She calls it her Mexican casserole surprise." He smiled. "It's not all that much of a surprise. I watched her make it once before. It has corn tortillas, shredded chicken, Ortega chilis, and like three cheeses… cream cheese, cheddar cheese, *cotija* cheese, and sour cream. I promise, it's divine."

"That's a lot of cheese."

"Well, I did just catch you eating cheese, so I'm going to guess you're not a vegan, like the lady of the house."

"Actually, that was soy cheese." I swiped at the air. "I just meant I try not to eat something so fattening."

"Really?" He raised an eyebrow. "Last time we hung out, you ate a cherry Danish, and if I recall, you went back for some pumpkin bread and a sugar cookie."

"True, but I was super hungry. And sugar is different than fat."

"I'm pretty sure that sugar turns into fat."

"Touché." I laughed and waved a hand toward the casserole. "Fine. Go ahead and warm up the goopy surprise."

He winked, walked to the cupboard to withdraw some plates, then scooped some onto each one. A quick pop in the microwave, and the mystery meal lay ready to consume.

I'll admit, once cooked, it smelled much better. Actually, it smelled yummy, like melted cheese, cooked tortillas, and Mexican spices. I timidly brought the first bite to my mouth and nibbled the end.

"Well?" he asked, having already eaten half of his portion.

I nodded. "Yeah, okay. It's good."

"I knew you'd like it."

"Okay, I lied. I don't usually avoid fattening food, and I have a bit of a sweet tooth."

"Nah," he said sarcastically. "I hadn't noticed."

"But I have an amazing metabolism."

"I noticed that, too." He let his gaze roll down my figure with a glimmer of humor in his eyes.

"Ha!" I slapped him playfully on the arm.

He laughed, pretending to squirm away.

I scraped the bottom of my plate, before serving

myself some more. It really was good, and before long, I had eaten three and half servings.

"Rosa told me you have some sort of amnesia. Is that what you were trying to tell me when we went for coffee?"

I hated to lie to Henry but knew I had no choice. He would never believe the truth. "Yeah, I'm guessing I hit my head in the jail cell, and it's kind of wiped some of the past away."

He set his fork down and wiped his mouth on a napkin. "This might be bad to say, but I'm glad."

"Glad I got hurt?"

"Glad, because I like the new you more."

I looked up from my empty plate. His beautiful chocolate eyes made my heart skip. Could he actually like me? No one ever *liked* me. In the past, men used me. Women hated me. Children feared me. And family, well they barely tolerated me. I hadn't had a real friend in as long as I could remember. I offered a soft, closed-mouth smile. Not knowing how to really react to this moment, I decided to go with what I did know, insults. "Maybe I never liked you either."

"I didn't mean to offend you."

I set my fork down and crossed my arms. "So, you didn't like the old me at all, huh?"

"Well, you didn't make it easy," he replied.

"I suppose I can give you that." I turned to the fridge and snagged a bottle of root beer. I didn't know if staff was supposed to drink them or not, but I had requested they always be stocked before. So, in essence, these were mine. I handed him one. I screwed off the top and held the bottle out. "To a better me."

Henry clanked the neck of his bottle with mine.

117

"To a better you."

I sipped. The sugar tasted amazing going down. Again, it took me back to a presence that no longer existed.

He set his bottle on the counter and folded his arms over his chest. "Do you have plans for the rest of the day?"

I brought the bottle to my chin, blew in the hole, and pretended to think. "Um, well, let's see. Does staring at the ceiling, taking a few more naps, and showering count?"

"Great, it's settled then." He picked up my empty plate. "I suggest we get out of here and go to the beach. We're having a Santa Ana, so you know what that means?"

"Hot desert wind."

"Well, yes, that. But what I meant was, it means we need to drive to the coolest part of the city. We need to go to the beach."

"We *need* to, huh?" I laughed.

"Yes, this qualifies as a need. You game?" He smiled. His straight teeth glowed against his bronzed skin.

I loved the beach, and the company would not be too bad either. And let's be real, anything would trump this depressing place. "Yeah, that would be cool. Oh, but wait. I have one problem."

He raised an eyebrow.

"I don't have a bathing suit."

"Hmm…let me text Eunice. You two are about the same size."

Before, that comment would have sent me over the edge. Now, I was extremely thankful. I had borrowed a few of her things already. For some reason, in this alternative universe, my fairy godmother didn't think to set me up with anything but a maid's uniform. And she thought *I* was evil. "Let me go shower, and I'll meet you back in half an hour?"

He nodded, texting on his phone. "If I am able to get you a suit, I'll have her leave it by your door."

"Cool, thanks." I walked back to my room, ready to get out of here.

Eunice met me by the bathroom with a black bathing suit and a teal maxi dress. Her scowl indicated she was less-than-thrilled to help, but she still held it out. I didn't get her. What she did and how she did it always conflicted. Such a mystery. Maybe this was part of her "choosing joy," who knew?

"You know, Cindy. I think when we get paid tomorrow, you might want to think about buying some of your own clothes. I can't keep giving you mine."

"Good idea," I said, taking the clothes. "Thank you. I really appreciate it."

She nodded, then pranced back down the hall and out of sight.

I showered and threw on the garments. I didn't really need thirty minutes. More like fifteen. Getting ready used to take me two hours. Now, I was only allowed ten minutes in the shower, and I had no makeup or hair products to worry about. Other than borrowing a plum lip gloss and a vanilla lotion from the drawer, I had little to do.

In my bedroom, I turned on a floor fan and held my hair upside down and raked my fingers through it. This would at least give me some volume. I didn't have a brush either, so this would have to do. I flipped my hair back. Luckily, the layers made it somewhat presentable. I would obey Eunice though. As soon as I had money tomorrow, clothes and toiletries were essential. A week without them had been torture.

Someone knocked on my door.

I opened it, and my breath caught.

Henry wore black board shorts and sandals. His taut tank top revealed a six-pack and muscles, but my gaze locked onto the dragon inked on his left bicep.

"Do you like my tattoo?"

My cheeks heated. "Yeah, it's cool. A dragon? Any significance?"

He pushed his bicep out, and I could see the full extent of the artwork. The black-and-white medieval dragon curled around his arm, horns on its head, and a red eye, with folded wings. A sword with a drop of blood pressed into the animal's heart. "Oh, it's wounded."

A playful twinkle danced in his eyes. "Yes, it's about living a life of honor and defeating those things that seem too big. A knight always has to defeat the dragon to win the princess's hand. Why do you think that is?"

"To prove he was a big and strong man?" I teased.

"Um, sort of, but not exactly." He chuckled. "The dragon was always a beast that threatened everybody. Only the brave could defeat it. If a knight could prove himself worthy of such a task, then the King would say he was worthy of the princess."

"Have you defeated your dragon?" I touched the sword on his arm.

But he didn't flinch. A soft grin slid across his handsome features, and his stare locked with mine.

"I'm working on it. I guess I'm not worthy yet."

We stared at each other for a moment. My pulse increased. I swallowed, not sure how to process what I felt. "Well, I like it. Ready?" More like, ready to change the subject? This man had done something to me. I hated to admit it, but I liked him. A working man. How could I have feelings for a blue-collar worker? But I did. *Insane*.

Of course, how could I not? He was super nice, even when I wasn't nice in return. He had rescued me a ton of times. Even before I became a pauper, he'd been my hero. And let's face it, the man could light a forest fire with his appearance. If I needed to be good, my first target would be him. I found when I was with him, I wanted to be good, to be better, and to be nice. Weird that he could affect me that way. Okay, it would be weird if anyone could affect me that way. I never expected to like anyone...or for anyone to ever really like me. Maybe I wasn't a complete and utter reject.

To our fortune, the LA traffic traveled faster than its usual snail's pace. The drive from the house to the beach took only twenty-two minutes. In the distance, the iconic Ferris wheel jutted high above the Santa Monica pier, surrounded by glowing florescent lights of every color. The parking lot buzzed with people and cars moving in and out. After four passes, he finally spotted an open slot and seized it.

"Looks like everyone had the same idea today," I said.

"I mean, ninety-degree weather on a Sunday in the middle of November. Who would want to go to the beach for that?" He winked.

We both laughed.

Henry exited the car and walked around to let me out.

As I rose next to him, I thought of the day he and I first met. He had smiled by the car, and I was mean because he didn't open my door. *What a jerk, I was.* Now, our stares locked, and I once again felt an intense attraction course through my body. It scared me, so I looked away.

"Do you want to go straight to the beach or up on the pier for a little bit?" he asked.

I had no money, and I could smell the caramelized sugar from here. What could I possibly do on the pier but drool at all the yummy treats? "The beach is fine."

He opened the trunk, pulled out a red cooler and tan blanket, and then guided me down to the ivory sand. Prone bodies on colorful towels dotted the entire coastline. We weaved our way through them, in search of an open space. Some tanned, and others relaxed under umbrellas. Kids and dogs ran in and out of the water, while adults chased both. Young handsome guys flirted with women in bikinis, and the older men ogled from afar. Farther out to sea, surfers fought for the next wave, and kids bobbed in the water, running with the tide.

The sand seeped into my torn shoes, so I removed them and walked barefoot along the shoreline. The granules percolated between my toes, warm and supple, with every step. I tried to take it all in. The gentle ocean breeze as it hugged my skin and calmed my nerves. Majestic waves folded and crashed in front of us, surely lulling the masses with their soothing sound. The smell of salt and sea fanned the air. I breathed deep, realizing for the moment, I was no longer a maid, just a young girl on a date with a hot guy in Santa Monica, California. I embraced the normal and relaxed sensation I felt.

"You okay?" he asked.

"Never better." I grinned.

After a ten-minute walk, we found a patch of sand. Henry flapped open the blanket, and we reclined on it. He removed his shirt.

It took everything in me not to stare. Every dark muscle cut into his stomach, prominent and hard. To divert my attention, I removed my dress. Never in my life had I worn a one-piece bathing suit. The plunging neckline and high cut on the hips made it bearable, but I preferred a bikini.

Henry grinned. "Would you like a root beer? I grabbed a few from the fridge."

"Sure," I answered.

He reached in the cooler and tossed one over.

I caught it. In the hot sun, the icy bottle was cold and soothing. I ran it over my arms and face, then unscrewed the cap and sipped from the lip. For a long while, we sat there, silent, drinking our root beers and staring at the crashing waves and the tide as it pressed in and out. We didn't really need to talk. Just be. His presence pacified me. My life usually sucked. But right now, in this second, it didn't. Even before all this fairy godmother madness, I had not experienced this much peace. Or anything close to it. I wanted to thank him... to hug him...to kiss him. As if he could read my mind, he glanced at me.

I offered a coy smile. Usually, that gave the guy a green light. But Henry either didn't notice or ignored it, got up, and offered a hand.

"Want to walk down to the water?"

"Sure." I shifted my bottle into the sand, raised my arms, and he took hold of my hands and lifted me to my feet. Our faces were now inches apart. My heart pounded, and for a moment, I thought he might kiss me.

But again, he let go and moved to my side.

Together, we strolled down to the water. The beach at the water's edge felt both chilly and firm under my feet. Waves licked at ankles, in and out, bubbling and hissing. With it, the ocean brought wildlife to the shore. A few times, I had jump out of the way of the lines of seaweed lapping at my toes. As the water receded, the sand tugged at my footing.

A seagull landed a few feet away and dunked his beak in the water, then flew away with something in his mouth.

Henry and I waded in a bit deeper to our hips. The waves moved our weight, and I caught Henry's elbow to keep from falling backward.

His arm slid around my waist and lifted me back.

"Thanks," I said, shyly.

He winked and let go.

We strolled back to the water's edge. Henry reached down to pick up a purple sand dollar and chucked it back into the sea.

"Nice, you saved one."

"Have you heard the story about the boy and the sand dollar?"

I shook my head.

"A boy walked down the shoreline, tossing the sand dollars back in the sea, and a guy came up to him and said, 'You know, you'll never make a difference. There are hundreds of sand dollars all along this shoreline.' And the little boy bent down, picked up another one, and tossed it in the ocean and said, 'It made a difference to that one.' "

"I like that."

"I'm surprised you've never heard it before."

I wasn't. Who would tell me a story like that? I had no friends. Well, until now. I cupped a hand over my eyes and squinted to see him in the bright sun. "Tell me your story. Where do you come from?"

"My story?" He touched a knuckle to his chin and then fanned his hand out. "Well, I'm originally from San Diego. My parents lived a modest life there. My dad worked security at Balboa Park, and my mom was a pre-school teacher. Then about ten years ago, he decided to move to Colorado to start his own business. So, I went to high school in Colorado, and then came back to So Cal after graduation."

"Why did you come to LA?"

"Why'd I come LA?" He faced me, squinting in the bright sun, with water dripping from his gorgeous face and chest. "Probably for the same reason most people do."

"To be famous?" I lifted an eyebrow and smiled.

"Close. To get into the movie business. I want to sell my screenplay."

My smile faded. "Your screenplay?"

"Yeah, I've been trying to get someone to read it for a while now."

I stared, afraid to ask this next question. If he answered the way I feared he would, the magic of this date would be over. "And you took the job with Mr. Tremaine as his limo driver because—"

He laughed. "Why do you think?"

It wasn't an answer, but the implication made me suddenly ill. "You hoped to pitch to my dad."

"Your dad?" His forehead crinkled.

"Sorry, Mr. Tremaine."

"Yeah. Hopefully, the opportunity will happen soon. Rosa said I should just leave it on the seat in the back of the limo, but I'm not so sure. That kind of makes me nervous."

"I don't feel so good." I turned for the shoreline and ran back to our blanket.

He followed. "Are you okay?"

Oh, how I hated people using Dad. It always infuriated me. Whether my dad knew me right now or not didn't matter. I was still protective of him. And this guy—his limo driver, whom he trusted—waited like a panther ready to pounce at any moment. My father deserved to have a few places where he could enjoy his peace without moochers and leeches—his own home and car. Not to allow him to have that; well, it made me livid. "I'm feeling sick. I'm ready to go." It was the truth. The idea of Henry right now made me want to vomit.

"Oh, okay." He reached the blanket, flapped it out to remove any sand, and then folded it and tucked it under his arm.

In an effort to leave faster, I grabbed the cooler and sauntered up the embankment. The sooner we left, the better. One reason—well, certainly not the only reason—but one reason I avoided friendships stemmed from this exact problem. I had always wondered if people really desired to be my friend or if they just wanted to get to Dad. Sure, Henry sought to be my friend. But like a wolf in sheep's clothing, he would betray my dad's trust. I should have never tried to let him in or to be his friend. People sucked and could not be trusted. They always coveted more than they deserved. It infuriated me beyond reason.

Henry tried to talk on the way home.

But I only offered grunts of "mmhmm" and "uh-huh" the entire way. I sensed his stare and his confusion. But I had no desire to explain, and he didn't ask. The perfect solution. I just wanted to shower and return to my solace. Better to be alone anyway.

Chapter Fifteen

Later that evening, Henry invited me to dinner.

I had no desire to see his face, because right now, it made me angry. How could I have let my guard down? Everyone sought something from my father. Now I knew, even Henry could not be trusted. So, I declined his invitation, claiming I had heat exhaustion and just needed to rest and drink lots of water. Luckily, he bought it and let me be.

Once I heard his car roll out of the driveway, I tiptoed into the kitchen and ate another plate of Rosa's Mexican surprise. The family, or should I say, *my* family, had decided to go away for the weekend and took Eunice along. Rosa, and most of the other staff, lived in their own homes, so the mansion was vacant except for one—me. I roamed from room to room, petting the furniture as I walked through. The large foyer, the formal dining room, the living room, the library, but I halted just outside Dad's study. As a child, I stayed in this doorframe until he beckoned me in. When famous or important people sat in the high-back leather chairs, he did not beckon, which became my cue to go on my way. But most of the time, he greeted me with his wonderful smile, and I would run to climb into his lap.

Unexpected tears pooled in my eyes. I sniffed and swiped them away with my sleeve and shuffled

128

forward. I crossed the threshold for the first time in years, and for a moment, guilt weighed on me. When my dad wasn't here, this space had always been off-limits. Probably because at age two, I sat quietly in the middle of his office, ripping pages from a first-edition book. I don't even remember the book's title, but I recall the stern warning about entering his study alone ever again.

I pushed the feeling of guilt away and toured the room. I reached out and grazed the bookshelf packed with old, gold-lettered reference books and modern-day biographies. The center sill boasted an Oscar and Golden Globe for Dad's production of his movie, *Thunder Apocalypse*. I touched the base of the tall, gold man. Shamefully, I never saw Dad get the award. When I found out that he invited Meredith, instead of me, to share his big moment, I spent that night drowning my sorrows at the bar.

I turned away to a large cherry desk positioned in the middle of the room. I dragged a finger across the side and landed at a picture of Meredith smiling. I stuck my tongue out and folded the frame onto her face.

Fancy pens and a gold letter opener lined up with a laptop and desk calendar. On the other end, I thumbed through a stack of screenplays that waited to be accepted or rejected. In front of the desk were two leather armchairs, separated by a coffee table. I dropped down into one and breathed deep in Dad's smell—spicy cologne and spearmint gum.

A memory filtered through my mind of Dad sitting in this chair next to a famous actor, who I had a huge crush on at the time. I peeked in, hoping I would get the green light to enter. Dad clearly pretended not to see me, which should have been the clue to leave, but I remained steady, waiting and hoping for an introduction.

After about ten minutes, the actor started to leave. He spotted me and smiled.

Of course, I was eleven, and he was like eighteen, so the smile on his part was innocent—but for me, it was everything. I grinned at the memory and got ready to leave.

In the hall, I shut the door, then sauntered to the stairs and stopped. I glanced from the bottom to the top—the forbidden climb to the second floor. Eunice served this area, not me. Technically, I had no right to be up there. Well, according to everyone but me. Of course, I had a right to be anywhere in this house, not that any of them realized it. The last time I showed on the second floor, Meredith about had my head. I took a deep breath and made the climb.

A high glass railing stretched along one side of the hall, making it possible to see the house below without falling. The other side displayed movie posters from Dad's various film projects. A single painting hung in the middle of them. Mom insisted that not everything be about Dad's work. She had purchased her favorite artist, Leonid Afremov. The bright and colorful painting of streetlights mixed with trees looked out of place among the Hollywood posters, but it made sense for anyone who knew her. It surprised me, that despite Meredith's presence, the painting still remained. Maybe Dad had the same idea and taste as Mom. Or maybe he couldn't bear to take it down. In this reality, Dad might not remember a daughter, but he still had a first wife.

Most likely, Meredith had no idea of the painting's

significance.

No matter the reason, I was glad to see it still hung there and at least one thing had not changed. I peeked inside my once bedroom, now a converted to a game room. Though altered, it felt right and comfortable to be here. I crept in, closed the door, and tiptoed to the window. Bulky white shutters had replaced my flowy chiffon curtains. I pulled the string to draw them open and peered to the driveway below.

From this vantage point, everything appeared to be as it had been before Dad's birthday wish. Many times, over the years, I perched in this window, waiting for his car to return from his latest trip. Right here, it all seemed the same. Intending to linger in that moment for a while longer, I turned my gaze to the room and found a beanbag. I positioned it at the window and plopped down. The air shot out and made a funny sound. I smiled, then stared out at the driveway, remaining for a while, pretending everything had returned to normal. My imagination soared, and I encouraged it.

I fantasized Mom saying from the doorway. "Hey, girl, what are you doing?"

"Oh, you know, just sitting here in the window, waiting for my Prince Charming to come and rescue me from this crazy existence," I responded.

Her ghostly image joined me in a phantom beanbag chair. She touched my hand and grinned a reassuring smile. "Someday, dear."

"I'm just so tired of being alone, Mom."

"Aw, my beautiful daughter. I promise, you won't always be alone."

"Are you sure? Because it sure feels that way since you left." Tears flowed down my cheeks. My chest heaved as I released years of pain. I refused to stop the grief this time. It needed to get out. I envisioned my mother pulling me into her arms, stroking my hair, and whispering things like, "It will be okay, Sweetheart. I promise."

"I love you, Mom. But I don't know if it'll ever be okay."

"Why do you say that?" she asked.

I pulled back and stared at the ghostly image. "Because I've been so bad and have basically destroyed everything."

She nodded with pinched lips, then her smile returned. "Nothing is permanent, Cindy. Sure, you made some mistakes along the way, but nothing is so messed up that it can't be fixed." Her finger tipped the bottom of my chin. "There is still time to change, my darling daughter. To make everything right."

"I don't know, Mom. I'm not the girl you left behind. I'm a monster. I've become evil, and darkness invaded my soul. You have no idea what I've done. If you did, then you'd totally get my concern. I'm afraid I can't be good. And if I can't be good—" I sucked in a deep breath against the knot forming in my throat. "What if I get stuck here? In this life? Forever. A maid." I sobbed, hard.

She reached out her invisible arm and wrapped it around my shoulders. "Then you'll make the best of this life—that really is the key, you know. I wish you could see that life isn't about *stuff*. It's about love. It's about people. Stop torturing yourself and everyone around you. Drop the bitterness and find joy."

There it was again, that word *joy*. I cried, unsure. "I'm just so angry, like all the time."

"I know."

"I don't want to be," I admitted.

"I know that, too," she said. "I love you, and I am proud of you."

"Proud of me. No, Mom, you could never be proud of me. This is something I am pretty sure of. I haven't been the daughter you raised. If you were to really show up outside my imagination, I'd be ashamed." I sniffed. "Didn't you hear me? I've been awful."

Her indistinct hand touched my cheek. "You're not dead yet. There is time to change that. To find a way for me to be proud of you."

"I want to."

"Then do it."

"I'm not sure I know how."

"Sure, you do. It's there, inside you, the sweet girl in front of the mirror. You just need to find her again."

I choked on my tears, then grinned and nodded. "For you, I'll try."

"No, Cindy. Do it for yourself first."

The sound of tires crackled below, and Mom's presence faded away.

I wiped my face with my elbow and glanced out to see Dad's luxury car was now parked out front. *Oh no, they came back early.* I should run back downstairs so I don't get caught on the second floor, but I had to see him first. I could bolt the minute Dad got out of the car.

First, Meredith stepped out, and then her girls.

And finally, my father exited. He grinned at them.

The smile I counted on, the one I missed so much. This was the first time I had seen him since our birthday party. He looked good and rested.

He started to walk around the car, but then stopped

to answer his cell phone. He held a finger up to Meredith, indicating he'd be just a moment.

I watched him as he lingered at the car, talking animatedly, likely bartering some deal.

The keys jingled below, and then the front door opened. *Oh no!* I had forgotten to run. Nothing blocked my path between here and the servants' quarters. If I left this room, they would see me.

Footsteps sounded on the stairs.

Panicked, I leapt for the closet. The built-in drawers and racks made it impossible to really hide, but then I remembered a secret cupboard in the middle island. I used to hide things in there. I inched my finger below the wood until I hit the nail. It released it and glided the access to the side. Once open, I crawled in and slid the door back. It was a tight squeeze and smelled of pine and dust. Not to mention, little air flow made it stuffy, and I had to stay in the fetal position. I closed my eyes and concentrated on my breathing in an effort to block out the discomfort and claustrophobia.

The two other rooms sandwiched mine, so escaping would not be easy. Within seconds, pop music blared from the girls' room next door. It occurred to me, despite my non-existence in this new reality, neither of the sisters had claimed this room. There were also several guest rooms downstairs. *Curious.* Why would they want to share a room when they could have their own room?

Low tones of Meredith and Dad conversing on the other side of the wall filtered through now and then. At some point, I fell asleep. When I opened my eyes again, the house had calmed to silent. I shoved the cabinet door aside and scrambled out. My muscles locked, and for a moment, my wobbly legs struggled to stand. I shook them, then tiptoed to the door. It stood ajar. Someone had come in here for some reason. I listened for a moment before slipping out. As it settled for the night, the mansion moaned and creaked. Each noise and tick made me jump. I crept to the stairway and touched my foot against the first step. It squeaked in complaint. I closed my eyes and inhaled deep. I started to take another step when I heard, "What are you doing up here?"

My heart leapt out of my chest. I glanced back to see the short and round outline of Charlotte standing behind me. Her frizzy red locks stuck out in all directions and zit cream glowed against her skin in the dark space. "I, um, brought something up for Eunice, but I'm going back to my room now." I turned to start going again.

Charlotte walked closer. "Then why are you sneaking around?"

"Well, I didn't want to wake anyone."

The girl crossed her arms and leaned her hip against the rail. "What did you bring up?"

Think. Think. What had I seen in the room? "Oh, a table tennis ball was found on the first floor. It must have got knocked down during a game. I just put it back. That's all."

Charlotte stared at me a moment, then her teeth glimmered in the night. "That was nice of you, but it probably could have waited until morning. I don't think any of us will be playing ping pong at 11 p.m."

"Yes, I suppose that's true." I laughed nervously. "You're Charlotte, right?"

"That's right. And you're Cynthia, the maid."

I bristled at the word *maid*. "Most people just call me Cindy."

"Cindy," she repeated. "Well, Cindy, my sister and I were just about to play a card game. You want to come play with us? It's always better with three people."

Part of me wanted to bolt. Play a game with the sisters? Was she nuts? The old me would have responded with a big fat "no" before the girl even finished her sentence, but perhaps I should. I could use the distraction and maybe, just maybe, this would work in my favor later. "Sure, why not? I suppose one hand couldn't hurt."

I followed her back down the hall. Not once had I ever stepped foot in their room since they had moved in. Before Dad remarried, it had housed Mom's art studio. It has always been cluttered, so I never went in. Now, I got why the sisters didn't care about sharing a room, or should I have said "suite."

Two loft beds adjoined at the corners of the room, covered by hot-pink-and-green comforters and matching pillows and stuffed animals. Underneath them sat a hot-pink couch and matching chaise. Two furry, lime-green bean bags rested on either side, and a round white couch sat in the middle of the room. The walls sported one canvas of ruby lips and another with a green eye and long black lashes. To my left lay a white dinette with fluffy green chairs.

Gabby waited in one with cards and a huge grin. "You found a third person. I'm so glad you didn't wake up Mom. She was super tired and a tad grumpy."

"Hi, I'm Cindy," I said, walking toward her.

"Welcome, Cindy. Sit, and we'll show you how to

play."

I slid into one of the green chairs—soft and comfortable, and my body relaxed.

Charlotte bent down to a short refrigerator, and then returned balancing three strawberry sodas, a bag of carrots, and a tub of hummus. "I hope you like strawberry. We adore anything pink. Don't we, Gabby?"

"Yes, yes. Of course. We like color. Really any color, but pink is the best. You can probably tell." Gabby beamed, peering around the room.

"Why do you suppose you're attracted to so much color? I've always been drawn to black," I admitted.

The two sisters glanced at each other, then Charlotte shrugged. "I suppose because it makes us happy. Both of us went through a pretty dark place when our dad left our mom. It was ugly. He never even said good-bye. He just left in the middle of the night, like we meant nothing to him, and I guess, we decided not to let the bad junk have us. We made a choice to just be happy."

Not once had I ever considered the sisters' past, pain, or feelings. It had not occurred to me that they also shared my grief of losing a parent. Nor had I cared. Guilt crushed my chest. Sure, I had never understood these two. I still didn't. But truthfully, I had never tried. For the first time, I did not view them with contempt, but I intended to see who they really were. Of course, if they knew who I actually was, I would apologize then and there, but an apology would not make sense in this context. So, I remained quiet, but thought, *I'm sorry, really and truly.* If I did make it out of this nightmare, I hoped to make it up to them somehow.

"Okay, enough talk about sad stuff. Let's play." Gabby fanned the cards through her fingers, then set them on the table, and lifted each one to explain its purpose. "The winner will be the one of us with the least number of points. But this is about deception. Charlotte has a tell, so I always know."

Charlotte huffed. "I do not."

"Sure, okay. You don't." Gabby smiled and winked at me. She finished the rules, then started to deal.

The game sounded easy enough, and it was. I won the first round.

"Beginner's luck," Gabby touted dramatically. "You haaave to play again. Please."

So, I did. Three more times. And I won three more times. This was my kind of game. Lie, be vicious, destroy your opponent—something I knew how to do well. I loved it.

"Wow, are you sure you've never played this game before?" Charlotte asked.

I shook my head. "Never."

"Well, you're really good at it. If we ever find a fourth, we'll have to play teams. I get you on mine, of course." Charlotte grinned.

"Hey!" Gabby said. "Who says?"

"Me, I called it."

"What are we, twelve? We'll play rock, paper, scissors." Gabby put out an open palm with a fist in the middle.

I had to smile at their chemistry and interaction. What I thought was nerdy and obnoxious before, I now saw as kind of enduring. "Thanks for letting me play. But I'd better get to bed. I've got an early day tomorrow mopping floors." I rose to go.

Gabby mirrored my movement and blocked my path. "This is strange to say, and please don't take offense to it, but you don't seem like someone who should be a maid."

I laughed, not sure how to respond. Of course, I didn't seem like someone who should be a maid, because I wasn't. "Thanks for saying so. I appreciate that."

"Don't sell yourself short, Cindy. I bet you could be someone amazing if you wanted to be. I mean, if you want to be a maid, there is nothing wrong with that. Like, if that is your dream, you can be the best maid, but I just think you are destined for more."

Charlotte came on the other side of me and put a hand on my shoulder.

Surprisingly, I didn't flinch her off.

"You're a strong young woman growing up in the twenty-first century. It's our time as women to rise above the stereotypes and become something amazing. Be whatever we want to be."

"Wow, that's, um—"

Charlotte stepped a bit close and laid a hand on my other shoulder. "What's your dream, Cindy?"

"My dream?" That stumped me. Did I even have one? I had never thought about it before. Life had been about spending my dad's money, not making goals. Why dream when one has it all? Because of our wealth, I had what most people worked their whole lives to obtain. Up until it was stripped from me, I had been all right with that. But if I didn't get my life back, what would I do? I had no idea.

"What have you always wanted to do when you

grow up?" Charlotte giggled. "*That* is your dream."

"Honestly, I'm not sure." Maybe now, I should find a dream and aspire for more. Because returning to my old life might not happen. Anything but being a maid. That I knew for sure.

"Well, when you figure it out, you let us know." Charlotte backed up a few steps.

Gabby let go. "Maybe we can help."

I walked toward the door, but then I stopped and twisted back around to face them. "Out of curiosity, what are your dreams once the two of you graduate?"

They looked at each other and said in unison, "To be like Oprah."

I stared a moment with a wrinkled brow; unsure I had heard right. "I'm sorry. Come again?"

Gabby flashed her metal smile and started pointing around the room. "You get a car, and you get a car, and you get a car."

"And you get a pony," Charlotte said, and both girls giggled.

I laughed. "Oh, you want to help people achieve their dreams."

"Precisely," they said in unison again.

It was like they shared a brain.

"There is nothing cooler than seeing someone sad start to smile for the first time," Charlotte said.

Gabby nodded, grinning ear to ear.

"We got to do that at an orphanage last year. Oh my gosh, it was the best ever." Charlotte rushed to a tiny bookshelf, removed a small album, flipped through it, and handed it out for me to see.

I cupped it in my palms and looked at the first photo.

A small kid sat in Gabby's lap, holding a sucker in his mouth with one hand and a large, plastic car in the other. Charlotte leaned forward and turned the glossy page to reveal a Christmas tree surrounded by presents, and then another photo of a group of kids tearing into them. "The best moment ever."

I really had misjudged these two. Sure, they were a little strange, but they were really nice people. I handed the book back. "That's super cool."

"We go every Christmas. You should go with us."

I grinned. "If I can get away, I'd like that."

"Cool," the girls said in unison.

"One last question."

"Shoot," Gabby said.

"Why do you two share a room, when there's another one just next door?" I asked, pointing toward my old bedroom.

Gabby shrugged. "I guess because we're used to sharing. Before coming here, all three of us lived in a studio apartment and had to split a queen-size bed. This house is so big, I suppose it just felt more comfortable to be together."

"Less scary," Charlotte added.

"I see." These two had something I never had—a person to go through the dark times with. How I craved that now. The sad realization hit me like a brick. Maybe if I hadn't been such a jerk to them, they would have given me that, too—friends to help carry the load. "Well, thank you again for letting me hang out with you both. It was a nice change of pace. Night."

"Anytime. Good night," Gabby said.

"Good night," Charlotte echoed.

I skipped down the steps, back to my room. Once

there, I crashed face-first onto my bed, exhausted from the emotional roller coaster of being angry with Henry, crying over everything, pretending to talk to Mom, and then laughing and having fun with those girls.

Strange enough, I kind of liked them, after all. They had an innocence about them and a happiness no matter what kind of attitude. I admired that. Unlike me, they didn't dwell on the negative. Despite losing their dad, they had a sunny outlook on life. I could use a little of their mindset. I closed my eyes and imagined a huge weight fall from my shoulders. For the first time since Mom died, I had a peaceful night's rest.

Chapter Sixteen

Around noon, the staff gathered in the kitchen for a pre-Thanksgiving lunch and a cake to celebrate one of the gardener's last days. Jorge and his wife had decided to return to family in Mexico for their golden years. Funny, I didn't even know Jorge that well. Honestly, I thought his name was something else like Bob. Apparently, he had worked for our family for twenty years. How did I not realize that?

"What's that in your hand?" Gus pointed to a long gold envelope in the man's right hand.

"Mr. Tremaine gave me a bonus check," Jorge said, wiping his eyes.

Sounds like Dad. Unlike me, he had an enormously generous bone in his body. I dipped my fork into the buttercream frosting and licked the tip. Everyone seemed merry, but I wasn't part of it. I observed from the corner like an outsider.

"Oh, good for him." Rosa patted Jorge's shoulder. "Well, we're going to miss you, my friend."

"Yes, me, too." Jorge touched her shoulder and turned to the room. "I'll miss you all very much."

The women all leaned in for a hug, and Gus wrapped around the outside. They all laughed and stepped back.

"We'll miss you, too," Rosa said. "But I'm jealous."

"Why?" asked Eunice.

"Because he's from Cancun."

Everyone hmmed and hawed.

"Yeah, you'll have it really bad, *mi amigo*," Rosa said. "I'd like to retire to Cancun."

"Come down any time." Jorge winked.

"I just might." She gave him another hug.

I focused my attention on the blue flower on my plate. I smashed it, then swirled it around, watching the blue mix with white lines. Behind me, I sensed Henry's presence. First, his cologne, then his footsteps. I couldn't help but look up, despite how much I despised him right now.

His gaze caught mine, and he winked.

I dropped my gaze back to the mound of colored sugar. I couldn't explain to him why he upset me. It wouldn't make sense. Why would a maid care about a chauffeur using the boss for gain? He didn't believe me about the alternative universe, so how could he possibly grasp my issue with him?

While the group gushed over Jorge, I tossed my plate in the garbage, slipped out, and returned to my room. We were given the rest of the week off of work to celebrate Thanksgiving. Dad usually let Meredith and her girls cook the traditional feast. The first year, Meredith served tofurkey, and Dad threatened to never allow her to cook again. He called her actions "sacrilegious and un-American." All in jest, of course, but she had been warned. So, it got a little better, but not by much. Her kind of cooking discarded the good stuff like cream, butter, or any kind of animal fat. You know, anything yummy. Everyone knew she liked her nutritious food, but who wanted to be healthy on

Thanksgiving? Just give me mashed potatoes with mounds of butter, stuffing, and gravy piled on top of all of it, and call it a day. But right now, I'd eat her tofurkey if it meant sitting next to Dad at the table. Instead, I would spend the holiday sulking in my room.

I nudged back the cheap curtain and stared out the window. The overcast sky edged shadows across my room, making it gloomier than usual. I lay down and stared at the popcorn ceiling, miserable, until someone knocked on my door. "It's unlocked," I said, lifting up on one elbow.

The door opened to reveal Henry.

Despite my irritation, his gorgeous looks still took my breath away. He wore dark pants and a white tuxedo shirt with the top button undone and the sleeves rolled up. Having discarded the jacket and tie, the white shirt pulled tight, exposing his muscles.

"Can I come in?" he asked.

I shrugged and pushed up to rest my back against the wall.

He crossed to the only chair in the room, flipped it around, and straddled the back. "I can tell you're upset with me, but I don't know why. Did I say or do something to make you mad?"

I stared into his gorgeous, amazing eyes, afraid to speak. I had never been afraid to speak my mind in an effort to avoid hurting someone else's feelings. Usually, I didn't care if people believed me or not. It had never been about them. Everything had always been about me. This, on the other hand, hurt. If only I could return to my old ways, protect my heart, and to stop caring. I longed for the simpler life. But then, I would never be able to return to my dad. And in truth, I had changed. I don't even know if the old Cindy existed anymore.

"Please say something," he said.

"I don't really know what to say, because you won't understand. You already don't believe me. So, what's the point?"

He folded his arms over the back of the chair and rested his chin on them. "Try me. I promise to have an open mind. No judgment. No denying your feelings. I will listen. Trust me."

Could I trust him? This guy who wanted to use Dad for his gain? But looking into his stare, I sensed I could. I folded my legs to my chest, wrapped my arms around them, and prepared to be honest. "It upset me that you planned to use Mr. Tremaine just to get what you wanted. People are forever using him, and it has always bothered me."

Without speaking, his gaze stayed on me a second.

I assumed he weighed his words, so I waited.

"Don't be mad," he finally said, "But I find it odd that you care, since you've only been here a short time."

"In your mind."

"In my mind?" He sat back, grasping the back of the chair.

I unfolded my legs and sighed. I needed to just dive into the deep end—sink or swim. "Look, I'm just gonna lay it all out there once more. You can call me crazy and leave, that's fine. I'm used to not having friends, so if that's what occurs, I'll deal with it. I so desperately want you to believe me, but I'm not counting on that happening. I've tried twice before. The first time, you accused me of dreaming again, and the second time, you told me to see a psychologist." I took a deep breath.

"Whether you believe me or not, I was born and raised in this house. Mr. Tremaine is my biological father. He was once married to my mother, who passed away from a brain aneurism when I was in high school. A short time after, he remarried Meredith. This is not a dream, nightmare, or anything like that. It's not psychosis or from me hitting my head in jail. This is real."

Henry shifted in the chair.

He seemed to be listening, so I continued. "After my mom died and my dad got remarried, I was furious. So, I was mean and nasty to everyone around me, including you. On my dad's birthday, he made a wish that I would change and be good or else. When he blew out his candles, everything transformed into this hell. Though it sounds ridiculous, a fairy godmother met me in the limo, and *poof*, I ended up here, a maid in this world...in your world." I paused to see if he was still with me.

His face was blank of any emotion.

But I still had his attention. "Of course, to make it more interesting, I have until midnight, at the start of the New Year, to have rehabilitated for the better, or I'll forever be a maid." I exhaled slowly as I lowered my gaze to my hands. I didn't know how he would respond. Though it might sting, I prepared my heart for him to get up and leave or to call me crazy. Because maybe I was. I only prayed he didn't do anything drastic, like have me committed. I had never been in a psych ward, but I was pretty sure I wouldn't like it.

The chair scraped the floor, and the bed dipped down as he sat. Henry reached for my hand.

I didn't resist. I raised my eyes to meet his.

"Call me the insane one, but I believe you," he

said.

My eyes filled with tears. I grinned, despite them.

"One question, though."

"Yeah?"

"At midnight, if you change back to your debutante self, will I still know you?"

I remembered the fairy godmother's answer. She had said I could not have both lives, but I didn't want to tell him just yet, so I lied. "I don't know."

He tucked a strand of my hair behind my ear. Our stares locked.

An invisible force lured us toward each other. I closed my eyes as his lips met mine. Soft and warm, he kissed me, then drew back.

"I'm sorry about Mr. Tremaine. I wasn't trying to use him, at least not intentionally. It has just been so hard in LA. I came out here from Castle Rock, Colorado, with nothing but a backpack, fifty dollars, and a screenplay. I've been trying to pitch my dream to anyone who would listen. After hearing of my million rejections, this buddy of mine said he could get me work for one of the biggest producers in Hollywood. Well, being a desperate man, I guess I just…"

I laced my fingers with his. "I get it. I'm just super protective of him, you know. But I don't think you're malicious."

He kissed me again. "I like you. I really hope you remember me when you change back into the boss."

I smiled. "I hope you remember me, too."

His finger trailed my cheek and chin, then his eyes lit up. "Hey, what are you doing for Thanksgiving?"

"You're looking at it."

He raised an eyebrow, then shook his head. "Uh,

no. You should come home with me."

"Home with you?" My pulse increased.

"Yeah, to Colorado. I'm leaving here in about an hour. Wanna go?"

"You want me to go to your parents' house?" I still couldn't believe what he was asking. A man taking a woman to his parents' house, that sounded serious. Maybe it wasn't. Maybe I overthought it.

"Well, my dad's house. My mom is no longer with us."

That bit of news overwhelmed me. Henry had lost his mom, too? We were more alike than I gave him credit for. "I'm so sorry."

He offered a tight grin. "So, what do you think? Road trip?"

Like I had so many offers. "Sure, why not? Sounds fun. Road trip."

Chapter Seventeen

As he drove through the mountains, Henry and I talked easily about life.

I confided in him about feelings that I had not shared with anyone about Mom, Meredith, and Dad. He listened, didn't judge, and somehow understood. In return, he did the same and confided in me. Both of us had lived similar paths, but our responses differed. I wished I had learned to grieve more productively. My life would have been sweeter. I definitely would not have landed in this situation.

About four hours in, we hit Vegas. We decided not to play tourist too much and get back on the road, but not before we snapped some pictures of him and me in front of the strip, the Luxor, Excalibur, and the MGM Grand. He bought me some hot toffee almonds and a large slushy for the rest of the trip.

A few hours longer, the desert landscape morphed into canyons and rock formations like I had never seen before. The sandstone fashioned into odd shapes of orange, red, and purple hues. At some point, I drifted off. I wished I hadn't. I'm pretty sure the landscape continued to be beautiful, but the long trip lulled me to sleep. I opened my eyes just as Henry pulled his vehicle in front of furniture store with an enormous red sign that read, *The King's Furniture and Upholstery*.

"Did you have a nice nap?" he asked, shutting off

the engine.

"Yeah." I ducked down to see out the front window and chuckled. "Are you in need of a couch?"

He leaned over and kissed me on the cheek. "This is it. Our house is behind the store. Come on."

I opened the door and walked around to meet Henry on the sidewalk. He led me to a path on the side of the brick store.

"My dad is the King," he explained. "And most people just call him that."

"So that would make you a prince." I laughed. "Well, I knew there was something to you always rescuing me."

He reached for my hand and smiled. "Come on."

At the back of the building revealed a beautiful, two-story brick house with double-paned glass windows and a French door. From this side, no one would assume it was attached to a storefront. Henry opened the door and let me pass by. Warm air and the smell of turkey hit us on entering. The foyer opened to a large living room—roomy with a stone fireplace. A big, white bear rug laid in the middle, and cowhide-covered chairs and matching couch rested in front, with a lack of a feminine touch apparent. *Definitely a man's cave.*

Henry lifted my jacket from my shoulders and dropped it on a rack by the door, then took my hand again and steered me behind the fireplace to a kitchen. The walls were painted forest-green, and the countertops and cabinets were decorated in a mahogany wood.

An older and darker version of Henry, with dark-silver hair and a gray beard, glanced up from a bowl of cranberries and beamed. "Son!" He dropped the spoon, wiped his hand on a towel, and embraced him.

"Good to see you, Dad."

They patted backs, then the King's gaze met mine, and he smiled. "And who is this beautiful lady you have with you?"

"Dad, this is Cindy. She works with me and…"

His father approached with arms outstretched.

Awkwardly, I filled them for a warm bear hug.

He stepped back, grinning. "And?"

"And Dad…" Henry slid an arm around my waist and drew me to his hip. "We're dating."

My heart flipped with those words. After twenty plus years, someone finally said I was theirs. Butterflies danced inside. I could have kissed him but refrained due to the present company.

His dad clapped, and then hugged us both again. "That's wonderful. Wonderful." He shifted back and pointed at his son. "Seems like forever, I have been trying to get this guy to date. He's just so stubborn. Got a mind of his own. You have to know, Cindy, my son won't date just anyone. You must be special."

I beamed. My cheeks heated. "Thanks, Mr.—"

"No, no mister. You can call me King. Everyone around here does." He grinned big and bright. "Wow, a real live girl, here with my son. That's the best news I've had all year."

"Okay, Dad. We get it." Henry laughed. "Sorry. My dad is always trying to marry me off." His face reddened, probably realizing what he had just said.

"My Henry is a catch. He deserves to be happy."

"Yes, I agree on both counts." I winked.

Henry and I eyed each other. His wavery smile

made me think he was a tad embarrassed, so I changed the subject. "How can I help with dinner?"

"Do you know how to shell peas?" King asked.

I laughed. "No, but I'd love to, if you show me." He handed me a bowl filled with what looked like pointy green beans and a smaller empty bowl.

He demonstrated tearing the stem backwards and opening the slit, before freeing the small green balls into the bowl.

Seemed simple enough. "Why not just get frozen or canned peas?"

King shook his head. "Oh, my, no, my dear. Fresh is always better."

And I believed him. I shelled, King cooked, and Henry made some special hot drink called watzil, or was it wassail? I wasn't sure, but it smelled amazing—apple and grape juice, cloves, oranges, cinnamon—and I couldn't wait to try it.

While we worked, we talked. I adored the King. I saw where Henry obtained his kind heart. King helped everyone in his community. People respected him. He had not remarried. Apparently, there were many prospects, but he loved his wife too much to even consider it. His mention of that pierced my heart. I wondered why my father had not been that way. It would have saved me a lot of heartache and maybe my attitude. "I struggle all the time with my dad remarrying. I don't understand how he could so quickly. Whenever I think about it, I get so angry."

King wiped his hands on a rag, and then touched my shoulder. "Everyone is different, my dear. Some people like me don't mind being alone. Others can't stand it. It's just too depressing. I loved a beautiful woman once, and that was enough for me. But you have to understand, that's not everyone's journey. We have to be careful putting our stuff onto other people. We are all different. Maybe your dad needs a companion. Likely, he felt lonely without one. Some people are just like that." He patted my arm. "If he found love twice, that's even better. Many are lucky to find it once. Twice is a miracle from God."

I reflected on his words as I released the last of the peas into the bowl. King could be right. My extreme extroverted Dad loved being around people. He always needed company. I couldn't think of too many times when he wasn't surrounded by others. And yes, I had put my expectations on him. Perhaps that wasn't fair.

But then, the redhead Meredith flashed in my mind. I still could not reconcile him picking her, but why she selected him had always bothered me the most. People used my father—desperate people, hurt people, but mostly, poor people. Meredith, a waitress, had nothing when he met her. Of course, she wanted him for his money. But then, I thought about her lifestyle. It had not changed. She still wore bohemian clothes off the rack, not designer ones. Her jewelry looked handmade, not expensive. She continued to drive her beat-up sedan, rather than drive the fancy new sports car Dad bought her last Christmas. She did say she'd drive an electric car if he bought her one, but that was just because she was a hippy trying to save the planet.

I walked to the sink to wash off my hands, still thinking it through. I looked down on Meredith, because I needed to, but I had never processed any of it. If she truly was after Dad's money, why did she continue to live like she did?

Henry came behind me and handed me a hand towel. "Penny for your thoughts."

"I'm just thinking about what your dad said. It's impactful."

"How so?"

"Talk about it later, okay?"

"Okay." He glanced at his dad. "I'm going to run to the car and get our bags. I'll be back shortly. Dad, don't start drilling her or telling her awkward baby stories while I'm gone."

His dad laughed. "You can trust me, son."

"I better." Henry kissed me on the cheek, then left.

"Here you go." I retrieved the bowl of peas and handed them to the King. "Need anything else?"

"Thank you, no. You can just sit and watch now. I'm close to being done."

"So, how did you get the name King?" I slid onto a stool at the counter. "Chicken or the egg?"

The man laughed a hardy laugh. "Definitely the chicken. When we moved here, my wife made a joke that a town like Castle Rock needed a king. So, when she passed away, I changed the name of my store to The King's Furniture in her honor. She would have loved it."

"And everyone just started calling you King?"

"Almost immediately. Started in our local newspaper and just grew from there. I knew it would make her smile, so I encouraged it." He pointed at the salt.

I slid it across the counter. "I like that I'm dating the son of royalty. It makes my man a prince."

King hooted deep from the gut.

I could not help but like this guy.

"And you, my girl, are his princess. I can tell by the way he looks at you."

That sent a shiver down my spine. No one had ever "liked" me…well not since Andy Scott.

Henry discarded our bags into some rooms in back, then helped carry containers and trays to the long mahogany farmer's table.

King carved the turkey and slid two slices onto my plate.

We passed around the mashed potatoes, gravy, cranberry sauce, and stuffing. Just when I didn't think I could fit more on my plate, King arrived with more. I scooped some sweet potatoes smothered in charred marshmallows on a small opening, then made room for peas, strawberry gelatin salad, and finished off with a flaky butter roll. After eating servant food for weeks, this piled-high heaven made me want to sing. I intended to eat every bite, even if it made me sick.

While we dined, we talked and laughed.

Henry spoke at ease in his father's presence. His dad shared story after story. Having lost his wife so early, they had obviously created a strong bond between father and son.

I recognized that well. I only wished I had longer with Dad. It could have solidified our relationship into this. What I witnessed today made me realize that the introduction of Meredith only caused division. My old feelings threatened to surface again. Even if she married him for the right reasons, it still hurt. Renewed rage for the redheaded hippy returned. I needed to be good right now, but I didn't want to. I craved revenge. Luckily, we were fifteen hours away. I could cool off before I saw her again.

Finished, we cleared the table, and King brought out some pumpkin pie.

I smothered mine in whipped cream.

King laughed. "Wow, you like the good stuff, I see."

"I like a little bit of pie to go with my whipped cream, yeah." I winked.

"Coffee?" he asked, walking to the pot on his stove.

"Always." I lifted my mug.

He crossed back to fill it.

"Do you have milk and sugar?"

He nodded and supplied me with both.

"Son, coffee?"

Henry shook his head, all but one bite of his pie gone. "I'm good."

King returned the pot to the stove.

With each bite of the pie, I calmed down a bit more. Sugar usually pacified the wild beast in me.

After dinner, Henry and I decided to take a walk.

I needed it desperately. Hand-in-hand, we strolled down the lazy town in front of the various storefronts, each closed for the holidays. The cobblestone streets and quaint buildings reminded me of a movie set in the 1950s. It was way more peaceful than the craziness of Los Angeles I endured day-to-day.

Henry guided us behind the main street to a small hiking trail. The smell of pine trees filtered through the air. No traffic, smog, or people to distract us—just silence and nature. The only sound came from the scraping of our shoes, the tapping of woodpeckers, and the cooing of doves. A slight breeze swept through the street. I pulled my jacket closer and tucked my hands in my pockets. "It's so beautiful here," I said, cutting the silence.

"Yeah, it was a great place to live."

"Do you ever miss it?" I asked.

He reached out his hand.

I slipped mine from my pocket into his.

"Yeah, a lot. LA can be a bit much."

"You think?" I giggled. "I mean…traffic, wall-to-wall people, fires, drought, high prices, smog, and backstabbing, dog-eat-dog aspiring artists. What's not to love about my hometown?"

"Most likely, if I wasn't trying to make it in the entertainment industry, I don't think I'd stay. How about you? Ever thought about leaving and going somewhere else?"

"No, up until this crazy fairy godmother debacle, I never thought about doing anything different than to live the life I was living." I glanced around at the rows of pine trees and the scampering squirrels. "But I could get used to this. Move to the Castle and live with my prince."

He stopped and pulled me into his chest.

His icy hand tilted my chin, and his mouth found mine. Our cold lips warmed. His arms wrapped around my waist, and he hugged me tighter. The kiss felt passionate, but sweet. We drew back and shared smiles.

"I happen to like you a lot." His gaze studied mine. "You know that, right?"

"The feeling is mutual." I pecked his lips with mine again. "You're stuck with me now."

His smile waned a bit.

Likely, he probably wondered if that was true. He now believed me, that I could disappear from his life on

New Year's Eve, well in its current state. He had shared with me on the drive; he feared a future like that. "Yeah, me, too," I said, reading his thoughts.

He kissed my nose. "So, explain before and during dinner. You said you had something to tell me later, and then you seemed upset when we were eating. What's up?"

Amazing that he could detect my frustration during dinner. He read me so easily. I had tried hard to hide it and not explode. But I guess years of wearing my heart on my sleeve had not done me any favors. "I'll start with dinner. It's hard to watch you and your dad."

Henry raised an eyebrow. "Why?"

"You are both so close. He didn't remarry like my dad did, and so you both had just each other for a long period of time. I wanted that relationship with my dad so bad. I never got it to that extent. I guess, it just hurts a little to see what I could have had, but I'm fine."

"To let someone new into your life is hard. But Meredith seems like she's a nice person. Maybe you could—"

Blood shot hot through my veins. I yanked back. "Now you're taking her side."

He held up his hands. "Whoa. I'm not taking anyone's side. I'm just trying to find you a silver lining, that's all. Something that doesn't involve you spiking her shampoo or plastic wrapping her toilet."

Despite how I felt, I laughed. I probably shouldn't have shared my prank ideas on the ride up here. "I can't guarantee those things won't happen."

A smirk pinched at the corner of his mouth. "I just want you to be happy. You know that, right?"

I reached for his hand and fastened it with mine.

"*You* make me happy. She doesn't."

"We don't have to talk about her then, if it makes you upset," he added, "But you said you'd tell me something later?"

So much for not talking about her. "I always assumed Meredith wanted to marry my dad for his money, but I started thinking about how she lives, you know, ugly clothes, cheap jewelry, and rundown car. None of that says 'marriage for money.' So, I guess I concluded that might not be true."

"Well, that's good, right?"

I was not in the mood to give her a pass. "So how about we enjoy our holiday and not talk about this anymore."

"Okay, deal." He slid a hand at my waist.

I rested my head on his shoulder and breathed deeply.

We remained there for a moment, both staring out at the snowy trees.

"Ready to go back for seconds? I think Dad also has pecan pie."

"I love pie, but it's the whipped cream that makes the dessert."

"I don't know, I think you could have used little more with your last serving."

"How about you just give me the tub and a spoon and leave me be?"

He kissed my nose. "Whatever you say, dear."

Yes, the way I liked it. Whatever I say. I laughed as we made our way back to the house for more pie and, of course, whipped cream.

Chapter Eighteen

Monday morning, we returned to work.

Rosa called all of the staff to the living room for a meeting.

A few additional people I didn't recognize lined up next to me.

The cook marched down the line, inspecting our collars, checking our uniforms, and examining our shoes. When she glanced at mine, she tsked. "Is that a tear? You need new shoes, Cindy."

"I know," I replied.

She shook her head and pivoted to face us. "Mr. Tremaine is coming back today on a 10 a.m. flight."

My stomach somersaulted. Dad was coming home.

"I want the house, the gardens, the limo, the food—everything tip-top shape, and we need to also get the house decorated for Christmas." Rosa kept talking.

Though her mouth still moved, she lost me at "Mr. Tremaine is coming back today..." I hoped to finally see Dad up close and personal in the flesh. How could he possibly look me in the eye and not recognize his own daughter? I wasn't sure if I felt excitement or fear. What if he didn't know who I was? I thought of him blowing out his candles without me. That devastated me, but at least, I still existed. The night of our birthday cut to the core, but he still remained my father. Sure, my pictures no longer hung on the walls, but I had to

161

believe, somewhere deep inside, this man would remember me, and that he loved me. He just had to *see* me.

"Cindy? Cindy?"

I blinked.

"Earth to Cindy. Are you with us?" Rosa asked, snapping her fingers in my face.

I blinked again. "Yes, sorry."

"I asked if you could clean the upstairs today. I need Eunice for decorating down here."

I nodded emphatically. The idea of returning to my room sounded good.

"Great, then we're all assigned. Lunch will be a little later today for obvious reasons. Dismissed." Rosa returned her gaze to a clipboard.

The crew dispersed.

I caught Henry's eye.

His expression held concern. "What's up?"

"He's coming back," I whispered.

Henry peered over my shoulder, then grabbed my hand and led me into the hallway. Once the door swung closed, he cupped his hands under my chin and kissed me.

Butterflies swarmed in my stomach.

"Sorry, I needed to do that first." Henry winked. "Now, who's coming back?"

"My dad. Do you think he'll recognize me?"

He pushed his lips together with a deep breath through his nose. "I'm here for you either way. If he knows who you are or if he doesn't."

I kissed him again. "Thank you. Now, I'd better get upstairs before Rosa fires me."

He brushed his lips to my forehead and sauntered

down the hall toward the outside exit.

I smiled and walked back in. After grabbing cleaning supplies from the closet, I climbed to the second floor. The vacuum hummed and the silverware clinked in other rooms below. I preferred the quiet upstairs. Meredith left for the farmer's market, and the sisters were in school. I had the second floor to myself for now.

I followed the glass railing to the end and opened the door to my parents' room. Nothing had changed. A four-poster, king-size bed rested in the center of the large room covered by a champagne comforter and matching pillows. Next to it, a pair of cherry wood dressers stood with matching mirrors. A cream chaise perched under the bay window, and a burgundy Persian rug partially covered the wooden floor. Over the bed hung a modern painting of the Hollywood sign that looked oddly out of place.

I meandered around the room, waving the feather duster at the furniture. When I reached the bed, I smiled. Many nights as a kid, I had pretended to have a nightmare, just so I could squeeze between my parents. Though king-size, I often took up more than eighty percent of the mattress, forcing Mom and Dad to ride the edges.

They never complained.

A hint of Dad's spicy aftershave hung in the air. I touched Dad's dresser and skimmed my hand along his brush. Two of his cufflinks glimmered in the sunlight that coursed through the windows. I lifted one up and studied the diamond at the end. I recalled him wearing these on our birthday. I set it back and continued to dust.

The door to the walk-in closet was ajar. I crossed to it and flipped on the switch. On the right hung all of my father's suits and shirts, but the left was almost bare with a few sandals, a pair of boots, and only one pair of dress pumps. On the rack, there hung maybe a dozen dresses—all bohemian, nothing fancy. This notion still baffled me. This woman had tons of money at her disposal, and what did she spend it on? A pair of sandals and a collection of peasant dresses? I would never understand her. Nothing in me wanted to try either. I might have found peace with the sisters and the workers, but not with her—not yet. She played some angle; my detective work just hadn't uncovered it yet. But I would one day. Somehow, I would expose her for what she was—maybe a screenwriter or struggling actress—and the truth would eventually come out. More digging would unearth the truth, and I embraced my new mission.

I snapped off the light and returned to dusting. After I finished, I vacuumed and cleaned the toilets. I reached for the trashcan, and my heart about ripped through my chest. A discarded pregnancy test lay on the bottom. With my rubber glove securely on, I withdrew the blue-and-white stick. My stomach churned, and I feared any discovery. I squeezed my eyes shut, brought the stick in front of my face, and peeked. The center of the plastic stick held a plus sign. Stars danced in front of my vision. I released the stick and reached for the wall, afraid to admit it. Meredith was with child. My *dad's* child.

I plopped down onto the seat of the toilet—stunned, numb, afraid to stand for fear I might throw up. If there existed a worst-case scenario, I had just slammed into it.

The sisters had said Meredith had news. They had said something about a new puppy, but was that all?

I had fed the dog, but maybe that wasn't the *real* news. Had this been what she had sought to tell me all along? She said she "wanted to get to know me better," but that seemed silly. Now it made sense. This was what she planned to share and to have said to my face, "You will be replaced."

I lumbered out of the bathroom, down the hall, and into my old bedroom. The sterile nature of the game room did little to help me find peace. I staggered into my old closet, dropped prone on the carpet, and closed my eyes. *Be good*, the fairy godmother had said. Did she know Meredith was pregnant when she said that? Couldn't she appreciate what that meant for me? How could I be good when Meredith kept creating a larger wedge between Dad and me? Not only had I been forgotten, and Mom had been deleted from our lives, but now, I would also be replaced with an "ours" baby. I wondered if she had told Dad yet. Did he know the night he made his horrible birthday wish? That just fueled my insecurity and more feelings of resentment.

Suddenly, I didn't wish to wallow any longer. I aspired to strike and get even, return to what I knew best, and be nasty. I walked into the game room and located all the table tennis balls, the disk in the air hockey game, and the foosball table ball. I dumped them in the garbage and wrapped up the bag. Of course, this probably wasn't the best form of revenge, but it gave me a certain amount of satisfaction. I stomped down the stairs, went outside, and tossed it inside the dumpster.

Across the lot, Henry caught my eye. He waved.

Without a response, I stormed back up the stairs and sprinted to my room again. I waited there until lunch time, not cleaning, but sleeping. I no longer cared about being fired. Let me live somewhere else, away from this madness.

At lunch, I kept to myself. No one seemed to mind or care. Afterwards, I returned to the second floor and finished my chores, only to keep from burning down the house. The rage that seared through my veins could easily send me over the edge. I knew right then, I was dangerous. *If the wrong person talks to me…Lord, help them.* I entered the sisters' room to dust.

"You sure are taking a long time up here," Eunice said from the doorway.

I glanced from the cloth in my hand and smirked. "And it's taken you since birth to pluck your eyebrows. We all work at our own pace."

She furrowed her bushy brow. "Excuse me?"

"No excuse for you, Eunice. You're just a mousy waif, working for people you aren't worthy to be friends with." I swiped a dust bunny onto the floor. "It's no wonder you haven't found a husband yet."

"Why are you being so mean again?"

"Again?" I pretended to dust the shelf. "I'll always be me. Just like you are who you are and don't seem to want to change. I'm mean. So, what? Deal with it."

The diminutive woman stared, mouth wide, obviously unsure how to respond. So, she didn't. She spun on her heel and disappeared out of my view. A moment later, the clomping of her footsteps could be heard down the hall as she descended the stairs.

A new emotion engulfed me. Never had I felt so

satisfied and so guilty at the same time. The power of being a jerk removed some of the anger, but Eunice had started to be nice. One might even say we were nearing friendship. Not best friends, but civil acquaintances with friend potential. Nothing I could say now would fix the hand grenade I just tossed in the middle of our relationship. This war now claimed a casualty. I sighed, unsure about who I was or what I sought to be. Most certainly my fairy godmother just red-marked my score card. In a single second, I probably sealed my fate. I would forever be a maid.

But the image of the pregnancy stick caused me not to care. I didn't know how to navigate these emotions in a healthy way. I had never had to before. I lacked any experience on how to be good when I felt anger. So, what could I do? So far, I had just resorted to what I knew. Be wretched. But it didn't satisfy me like before. In the past few months, I must have grown a conscience. The longer I dwelled on what I did, the worse I felt.

Tires crackled below. I rushed to the window and peeked out behind the blinds.

Dad emerged from the limo.

I tucked the rag into my waistband, glanced at my reflection, and attempted to smooth my hair and dress. I walked to the edge of the stairs, just as the front door opened.

Meredith waited at the bottom and hugged her husband as soon as he stepped inside.

Adrenaline coursed through my veins. He was here. I lingered, praying he recognized me. Hoping for a sign, a miracle, some register of expression that indicated he remembered me, but none came. When he peered up, his gaze looked right through me.

The two of them exited to the living room, arm in arm.

I trudged down the stairs and back to the kitchen.

Eunice sat on the stool, crying. Rosa patted her back. Both women glared at me.

Rightfully so. But what could I do? "I'm sorry, Eunice. I'm having a bad morning."

The waif sniffed. "You know, we gave you chance after chance, and all we get in return is nastiness. You're a horrible and damaged person, Cindy, and I hope you get what's coming to you."

Those words stabbed my soul. "I already have," I whispered and hurried past them and out of the kitchen to the solace of my room. I stayed there for the remainder of the day. No one bothered to check on me or give me more orders. I think for the moment, everyone thought that best. They were right. I was a horrible and damaged person. Likely, that would never change.

Chapter Nineteen

The weeks leading up to Christmas hurt worse than the beginning of my punishment. My mood fluctuated, but mostly stayed on "aggravated." I snapped, sneered, and basically alienated anyone and everyone I came in contact with. Thankfully, the sisters left for some fancy ski trip with their aunt and missed my wrath.

By the time Christmas break arrived, the staff bolted toward their cars. None said good-bye, likely wanting to distance themselves from me.

Not that I blamed them. I craved a vacation from me, too.

Henry might be the slight exception, but even he and I had had several fights lately.

He would remind me of the goal. I was to be better and to change. But my resentment for Meredith oozed an inky darkness deep into my heart. The agony steered every decision and action I made. I desired to change my attitude but was clueless on how to begin the process. I stepped out on the porch and stared as the last car pulled out of the driveway.

A moment later, Meredith drove in and parked. She stepped out of the car and glanced up at me. She didn't smile.

Neither did I. I sensed she knew how I felt about her. I overheard a rumor earlier in the week—she had tried to have me fired.

Dad stopped it somehow.

I never found out the how and why, only that she had orchestrated the discussion. How I detested her. As she passed out of my view, my attitude nosedived off a cliff. *God help anyone who talks to me right now.*

"Hey, there," Henry said behind me. "How are you feeling?"

"Who cares?" I snapped.

"That's not fair. I care."

"Do you? Or are you just like everyone else?" I spun around to face him, heat rising in my body. I should stop talking and walk away, but I couldn't. The desire to scream at Meredith needed to be released somehow, and Henry was my only viable target. "I bet you're hoping I'll remember you when this is over so I can get your screenplay in front of my dad? That's why you are trying to make me good, right? That's the only way I can help you is if I remember."

With pursed lips, Henry nodded once, turned, and left without another word.

Guilt engulfed my soul. I should run after him and apologize or beg forgiveness. But I couldn't yet. Not with the vile emotions coursing through my body at the moment. Right now, I needed to calm down. In the old days, I either drank or shopped. Since I no longer had an ID, shopping would have to do. I shrunk back to my room, collected what little money I had, and called a taxi to come get me.

I had the driver drop me off in front of Darren's Department Store. Shoulders back and head high, I strode inside and exhaled. A wave of familiar peace washed over me. Shopping therapy might be exactly what I needed. But within minutes of stepping into the store, the glares of store personnel followed me around the floor. Their attention could be because I wore knockoff blue jeans and a five-dollar T-shirt, or more likely, it could be because I stole from them before. Either way, they watched me like a hawk.

I closed my eyes and petted the silk scarves. It took me back. For a second, I became the old me. My expensive "friends" still loved me. They returned me to a world of luxury. To think I took all this for granted. No matter what, I don't think I would do that again. At least, that had changed. I appreciated it all. I stopped by the makeup and smiled at the woman behind the counter.

She responded with a plastic smile. "May I help you?"

"Yes, I would like to have a sample makeover, please." I hadn't worn makeup in so long, but I desperately needed to feel "normal."

"Do you have the money to buy anything?" she asked in a snooty tone and with her nose in the air.

I recognized this tactic. Make the person feel less than herself, so maybe she'll leave. But I would not be deterred by this approach. I had money from my paycheck, and I intended to spend it. I narrowed my eyes and mirrored her plastic smile, "Why yes, I do."

She pinched her lips together, held up a finger indicating she'd be back, and sauntered away.

I slid into the gold stool and waited to be pampered. I noticed a gold bottle of perfume to my right. I sprayed it in front of my face and sniffed. It smelt of vanilla and rain. I sprayed again and waved my wrists and neck into the mist.

The saleslady came into view behind the display,

tailed by a man in a suit, likely the manager.

I set the bottle down and turned to face them.

"This is her," the lady hissed in the man's ear.

She spoke loud enough for me to hear.

The balding man with glasses crossed his arms and glared. "You're no longer allowed to shop at Darren's Department Store, miss."

"Why not?" I countered. "I plan to buy stuff. I already told her that. I have money. I know I look like a hobo, but I promise you, I'm not."

The man stepped forward. "Once you've been arrested for shoplifting in our stores, our policy states we are obligated to deny you service. We need you to leave, or we'll call security."

I blinked, waiting a second for that to fully register. "Fine, no need to get all huffy. I'll go." So, my past had not totally been erased in this new reality. I guess I should have suspected that, since I did go to jail in this reality. I wondered, though, did they know me as Cynthia Tremaine, or did that name not transfer over? I vaguely remember them calling me something else. I sauntered out the sliding glass door leading into the main mall.

Rows of neon signs and Christmas decorations lined the indoor walkway. Holiday music and conversations echoed from the high ceiling. A few kids lingered against the rail, eating ice cream. Most of the people dashed in a hurry with shopping bags, and a few moms pushed strollers toward the North Pole.

Santa waved.

I waved back. I had only one memory of the red, fat guy. Around age four or five, Mom had me sit on his lap, but I cried, and she never took me again. Also, she told me the truth shortly after that, so I never got caught up in the magic.

I weaved through the crowd of little dreamers and into the vast sea of shoppers. The more I ambled down the tiled floor, the stronger the aroma of greasy fries and grilled burgers made my stomach rumble. The food court must be my next destination.

Well, so I thought, until I got distracted by a kiosk filled with colorful makeup. In the past, I wouldn't have shopped at this kind of place—off-brands and cheap merchandise—but since I couldn't shop in Darren's, I guess I had no choice. I thumbed through the products and purchased a light foundation with matching powder, a soft pink blush, a dewberry lipstick, smoky eyeliner, and a tube of black mascara, as well as a brush and hair spray. I handed the cashier two twenties and left with my purchase. I couldn't wait to find a corner to put it on. I needed the morale boost.

I reached the food court, and the angels sang in my head, "Aaah!" A large hamburger, curly fries, and a huge soda would certainly lift my spirits, too. I stopped in front of a large yellow arrow and peered up at the menu.

"Hello. What can I get you?" asked the man behind the counter.

"I'll have a cheeseburger, large fry, and—" I paused. "I'll have a small chocolate chip shake."

The cashier rang me up, and another lady handed me the order.

I turned with my tray and frowned at the vast amount of people eating. I snaked around the tables until I spotted an empty spot in the far back of the food court. Some dork left his trash behind, but I was glad it remained vacated. I stuffed the trash in the can nearest to it and used a napkin to wipe off the table and chair. "Even on my time off, I have to clean up someone else's mess," I muttered, as I rolled my eyes.

Finally seated, I unwrapped the burger and squirted some ketchup on the side of the paper. I brought the buttered bun to my lips and bit. *So good*. Each bite made me smile a little more, but I couldn't wait to put on the makeup. I prepared to start my makeover by spreading my purchases out on the table next to my food. I applied makeup between bites, only waiting on the lipstick. By the last fry, I felt like myself again. I applied lipstick, then winked in the compact mirror. If only cosmetics could fix a broken soul, too.

I needed to see Henry as soon as possible. He had not seen me look this decent the entire time he'd known me. Well, this me and I needed to make things right. I would stop and buy a few clothing items, then I would go find him and pray I hadn't destroyed our relationship beyond repair.

****

That night, I put on new jeans and a cream poplin top. I fixed my hair the best I could, touched up my makeup, and crept down the hall to Henry's room. My heart hammered in my chest. One thing I had never done before was apologize to people. I could see why. It felt extremely uncomfortable and humbling. But if I didn't, I would lose the one good thing I had in my life.

So, I swallowed what little pride I had left and tapped on his door. There were things I could not take back. I had questioned his motives for being here again. I didn't mean it. I acted out of ignorance on how to behave. Okay, that was a lie. It wasn't ignorance. My personality default setting was jerk, and it didn't seem to have much of an off switch.

The door opened to reveal Henry in gray sweats and a black tank top that showed every muscle.

Of course, you had to be hotter than ever... I gulped and tried to smile, happy he didn't slam the door in my face. "I'm so sorry for everything I said earlier." I lowered my gaze to my hands. My cuticles were a mess. My nails were short and ugly. I seriously need a manicure. *Stop thinking about your hands.* I peered up again. "Can I come in, please?"

Without speaking, he stepped back.

The move provided a space so I could enter. I glanced around. With the exception of better paintings, an ocean instead of eighties flowers, his room didn't appear much different than mine.

A few clothes lay discarded on the floor. Henry scooped them up and tossed them in the tiny closet, then waved for me to sit on the bed.

I perched on the edge.

He leaned his hip against the dresser with arms crossed, feet shoulder-width apart.

"Look, I know I owe you a huge apology. Honestly, I owe the world one. I don't know how to stop being so wicked. Right now, I am furious about the pregnancy. It's all I think about, and frankly, it's messing with my head."

Henry's expression remained tight. "You want to be good, then be good. Stop dwelling on Meredith. She's only one person, and you're allowing her to rule your life. Pretty soon, you'll be left in your bitterness and have no one."

I recognized that meant him, too. "I know." Fresh

tears grazed my new makeup. I dabbed my cheeks, hoping to preserve some of it.

His expression softened, and he lifted my chin with his knuckle. "I can help you, but you have to stop resisting, okay?"

I nodded and stood.

He wrapped his arms around me and hugged me tight. "And your makeup looks really pretty."

His breath hot on my cheek, I laughed through my tears. "Thanks. Well, it did until now."

He kissed the top of my head. "Still beautiful."

I sniffed. "Thank you."

"So, since you're all made-up, do you want to get out of here and go for dinner? I'm starving."

"Have you ever known me to turn down food?"

"Never." He grabbed his wallet. "What do you want to eat?"

"I had a burger for lunch, so how about Mexican?"

"Oh, yes, always a good choice. Let's hit Roberto's on Eighth. Best *carne asada* fries in the city."

I slid under his arm and squeezed his side. "I don't know if I deserve a man who will buy me a carne asada fries, but I'll take it."

****

After gorging on French fries smothered in steak, cheese, beans, and guacamole, we decided to take a walk on Hollywood Boulevard. Even though Dad was a big deal in Hollywood, I had never been down here. Henry intertwined his fingers with mine and led me down the heart of the town. Neon lights, music, and the buzz of the city filled the air.

The streets, packed with tourists from around the world, pressed tightly together in awe of the various names in their path. Several people dressed like famous celebrities danced, sang, or entertained for money.

I spotted Marilyn Monroe, Prince, and Judy Garland.

A Michael Jackson look-a-like moonwalked, spun around, tipped up on his toes, and squealed.

I laughed and tossed a few coins in his hat.

We meandered down the boardwalk, naming off the names of the tiled stars below our feet. I got most excited when I saw Anne Hathaway's star. "I love her. She came to dinner once when my dad was considering her for one of his movies."

"You've met Anne Hathaway?"

"Just the once. She's ubercool."

We continued to stroll, stopping at some actor that Henry liked who I've never heard of. Red Skeleton or something like that.

"Don't you think it's odd that people walk on your name, though?" Henry asked, stepping around his star and snapping a photo with his phone.

"Yeah, it is kind of odd, I suppose."

"But I guess it's also cool, because you know at some point, these people were right here."

I raised an eyebrow. "I wouldn't have thought about you being into all that."

"Isn't everyone?"

I shook my head. "You work in a Hollywood producer's home. A lot of famous people come through there all the time and have even sat in your limo. That's closer than these stars who are trampled on day-by-day."

He shrugged. "I guess."

When we reached the Chinese Theatre, Henry

snapped a few more photos. Some with both of us acting silly or kissing.

I stepped in the cement prints of Julie Garland and cringed. My feet looked gigantic next to hers. We talked and laughed. Everything felt light again. For one night, I would not allow my mind to dwell on my past, but only my present of the here and now. The best decision I'd made in a long time. On the way back to the mansion, I laid my head on Henry's shoulder. "Thanks, Henry."

"For what?"

"For once again, rescuing me."

Chapter Twenty

On Christmas Eve, Henry entered my room dressed in navy-blue dress pants and a blue-and-white-striped shirt. His cologne lingered fiery and alluring.

I greeted him with a hug and a kiss. "Well, you look nice."

"I wondered if you'd like to go to a Christmas Eve service with me."

"To where? Church?" I sneered.

He laughed. "You don't have to say it like that."

"I'm sorry." I licked my lips and said softly with mocked sincerity, "Are you asking me to church?"

"You're ridiculous." He smiled, touched my chin, and brought his lips softly to mine. "Yes. There's a church up the highway that has a Christmas Eve service. We sing carols by candlelight, and there is some kind of inspirational message about the season. A bunch of us go every year. I promise, you'll like it."

I bit my cheek, not sure if that was such a great idea. *I wouldn't be surprised if I caught fire the minute I stepped through the doorway of the holy place.*

"There're hot cocoa and cookies," he added with a wink.

"Oh well, if there're cocoa and cookies," I repeated with a touch of sarcasm.

"Seriously, you'll like it."

"When you say, 'A bunch of us go…' who are you

referring to exactly?"

"Um..." He looked down and shifted from one foot to the other. "The staff."

I waved at the air and stepped back. "Nah. That's probably not a good idea. They hate me."

He tucked my hand into his. "They don't hate you. Annoyed, maybe, but not hate. Look, you need to mend those fences. This is the perfect chance to do that."

I still wasn't sure, but I could tell this service meant something to him, so I should care and support him. "Fine, but only if we sit way in the back, away from the crowd. That way, when the lightning strikes, we don't kill a bunch of people."

He laughed. "Deal."

"How long do I have to get ready?"

"Five minutes?" he said.

"Five minutes? I can't wash my hands in five minutes." I reached for the red bell sleeve dress I had purchased with my paycheck and sprinted down the hall into the bathroom. I combed my hair, quickly put on some makeup, and stepped into the hall in a little over fifteen minutes. Henry waited, maybe impatiently, but when I stepped out, the huge grin on his face said it was all good.

Thanks to the lovely LA traffic, the trip took another twenty minutes just to get to the church down the road. The parking lot was full, so we drove farther and took the shuttle to the main entrance.

The amount of people put a lump in my throat. I had not stepped foot in a church since Mom died. What should I expect? Could they glimpse into my soul and see the true blackness of my heart?

Henry slid his hand into mine.

I squeezed it tight. We weaved through a crowd drinking coffee on the patio.

Just inside the door, a woman greeted us and handed me a small green sheet with Christmas carols printed on the outside.

The inside lobby buzzed with activity as people laughed, hugged, and conversed. Several men and women shook my hand. One older lady tried to give me a hug.

I, of course, made it awkward. Henry must have sensed my dismay, as he led me straight to the back of the sanctuary. As promised, we sat in the last pew in the middle of the auditorium. Once seated, I glanced around the enormous building. Five more rows were positioned to my left and a good forty in front on six sides.

Henry said a balcony covered us.

I kind of wished we had sat there, completely hidden and out of view.

People trickled in and slipped into the open pews in front of us. On the platform, various musicians tuned their instruments. Christmas trees lined both sides of the stage, and a row of poinsettias decorated the steps.

Several rows down, I noticed Rosa and Eunice take a seat.

Thankfully, Henry didn't beckon them to join us.

I held my breath and kept an eye on them.

A woman in the row behind them tapped Rosa on the shoulder. The older woman hugged her, and then spotted us over the lady's shoulder. She smiled at Henry, but her countenance hardened when she saw me.

The music started, and thankfully, she dropped back around into her seat. We sang carols and a couple of songs I had not heard before. The room rang of joy and peace. Part of me wanted to escape out the back door, while the other part of me wanted to fold into this sensation and never leave.

After the singing, we shook each other's hands.

Rosa and Eunice walked back and hugged Henry. They nodded at me but gave little else.

"Please be seated," an older man said.

I assumed he must be the preacher.

He prayed. "I want to read a verse you are probably all familiar with. We see it at ball games and sports events in the stands. It really is the Christmas story. Turn with me to John 3:16-18."

Some people flipped pages in Bibles in their laps.

Some people, like me, just stared at the screens.

He read from the Bible. " 'For God so loved the world that he gave his one and only Son, that whoever believes in him shall not perish but have eternal life. For God did not send his Son into the world to condemn the world, but to save the world through him. Whoever believes in him is not condemned...' " He closed his Bible and looked at the audience. "I want to focus on the word *condemn*. This season is a season of forgiveness. It is why Jesus was born, but it should also be a season of new beginnings for us. A chance to show our love for others. When you hold onto a grudge, you do not hurt the other person, you hurt yourself. Forgiveness will unburden you."

What the preacher said pierced my heart. He talked more, but I heard little else he said. I never realized that my bitterness for Meredith didn't hurt her at all. It only hurt me. I suffered, but not her. She walked in this life free, and I existed in self-afflicted pain. I needed release and to find the peace he talked about. I had to forgive her. I processed a ton of emotions in a matter of minutes: anger, hatred, sorrow, grief, contempt, resentment, jealousy, pride. I played everything over and over in my mind from the minute my mother hit the floor behind me until this moment in time. Meredith had never been anything but nice, but I treated her horribly, and yet, she continued to try. My resentment kept her at bay.

I could not continue to hold these feelings anymore. They hurt too much. They destroyed me little by little, and soon, I would be lost. I knew this, felt this, and believed this. Meredith one, me zero. My hatred for her slowly killed my soul. I had to let go. "Meredith, I forgive you," I whispered under my breath. Instantly, a weight lifted. I prayed silently for a while. I needed to alter my life and to express myself differently, to be kinder, and to ask for others' forgiveness.

People around me stood and started to sing again.

I slid out of the pew and walked to Rosa's and Eunice's row.

The devil on my shoulder asked, "What are you doing?" I imagined flicking him off and maintaining my course.

Both women glanced my way. The tears in their eyes said the message had moved them as well.

"I'm sorry," I said, glancing at each of them. "I know I've been awful to you and everyone else. I have been holding in some serious bitterness, and it affected how I responded to both of you. You didn't deserve any of it, and I apologize profusely."

The women joined me in the aisle and hugged me tight. The three of us cried.

The pain of my mom dying, the disgust of my dad's remarriage, and the hatred toward Meredith all seemed to melt into the carpet beneath my feet.

Henry joined me and led me out to the courtyard, where he handed me a napkin, a gingerbread cookie, and a cup of cocoa.

I used the napkin to wipe away my tears. I wasn't sure if I could swallow a cookie just yet.

"Are you okay?" he asked, before biting the leg off his cookie.

"Yeah, better than I thought possible." I sipped the warm drink. "Thanks for bringing me here. This is what I needed."

He gave me a side hug, just as Rosa and a portly man with gray hair approached us on the patio.

"Cindy, this is my husband, Pat."

He stuck out his meaty hand.

I shook it. "Nice to meet you, Pat."

"Likewise."

"What are you two doing tomorrow?" Rosa looked at both of us.

"Probably nothing." *My family doesn't know I exist, so what can I do?*

Rosa pointed at her husband. "Well, Pat and I are eating a Christmas brunch around 11 a.m. You're both invited, if you'd like to come."

Henry glanced at me.

I smiled.

"Sounds good," he replied.

"Do you still know how to get to my house?" she asked Henry.

"Up on Brady, right?"

"Yeah, the yellow house just behind the falafel

restaurant."

"Got it," Henry said.

"Great. See you tomorrow." Rosa tucked her hand under Pat's arm, and the two shuffled toward the parking lot.

Suddenly, I realized Eunice was there, also.

She gave an awkward grin, then scuttled off.

"I hope they truly forgive me. I've been so awful."

Henry took a sip of his hot chocolate. "They're nice people. I think they already have. You want to head back to the house?"

"Yeah." I tossed trash in a nearby can, then followed him to the car.

We didn't say much on the way back. Most likely, he sensed my emotional roller coaster and chose to give me space. Often when I had one, I could be mean. But something inside me had clicked off of the "jerk" setting. I felt different and transformed, and I only wanted to do things that promoted the new me.

Henry parked in the back lot, and we got out.

Meredith waited on the porch.

I wanted to promote the new me, but her presence challenged that.

"Can the two of you come here for a moment?" she asked.

I fought the urge to roll my eyes. The new me would take time, but it started with kindness. "Sure, how can we help?"

Meredith smiled. "I want to surprise my husband with a gift tomorrow, but I need your assistance in bringing it inside after he goes to bed. Would the two of you mind carrying it to the living room later this evening? It's in the garage with a big bow. You can't miss it."

We glanced at each other, then Henry nodded. "Sure."

"Thank you. I so appreciate it." She touched my arm, then walked back inside.

Mixed emotions poured through me, but I chose to hang onto the one focused on Meredith's generosity to my dad. She wanted to do something nice for him. I would focus on that. Forgiveness was not for the weak. Forgiveness required tenacity and decisions made each moment of every day. Forgiveness was a choice. I had to choose joy, like Eunice did.

Henry and I entered the staff lounge. I had only been in the tiny space once since moving in, mainly because the room looked like a garage sale. A brown faux-leather sofa faced a small wood-burning stove. Between the stove and the couch stood a small, smoked-glass coffee table with gold trim. To the left rocked an old wooden chair, and to the right, a beat-up orange futon clashed in its space.

We sat on the sofa, and he touched his lips to mine. "I have something for you."

My heart leapt. It had been a while since I had received a gift. I smiled, closed my eyes, and held out my open palms.

He laughed, then pressed something small in my hand.

I peeked out one eye, then both, and saw a small white box the size of his fist. *Please don't let this be anything too fancy.* I could not give him an expensive gift for Christmas, and I definitely wasn't ready to be asked an important question. My hand trembled as I lifted the lid. But all fear dispersed replaced with laughter.

Set on a fluffy cotton square lay a bottle of shoe glue and a packet of bedazzle rhinestones.

"You're too funny. It's definitely the right size." I wrapped my arms around his neck and squeezed tight.

"Well, my princess needed to fix her shoe, and I could tell you're the type of woman who could use a little bedazzle in her life."

"You know me well." I kissed him again. "I have something for you, too, but you'll have to wait until tomorrow."

His eyebrows elevated in the middle.

"Trust me?"

"A hundred percent." He crawled to the wood-burning stove, tossed in a paper log, lit it, and joined me again. For a moment, the two of us stared at the flames licking the paper, and then leaned into each other. In the background, sounds of Christmas music wafted through from the main house.

Meredith liked to blast Christmas music on Christmas Eve while the family gorged themselves on sprout cookies and soy eggnog.

Usually, I chose to sulk in my room instead of participating. But today, I would have come down with a merry attitude, sang along, and even devoured some of Meredith's nasty vegan treats.

Henry fingered a strand of my hair and stared intently. "I know I'm always asking you this, but are you okay? I mean, really, okay?"

"Yeah, for the first time, I think so. I am starting to realize what's important in this world, that's all." I shifted sideways to see his handsome face better. The fire light twinkled in his golden eyes and danced on his face, making his skin look like smooth peanut butter. I touched his cheek and grinned. "I'm really glad I found you."

"Me, too." His lips traveled from my forehead, down to my nose, and landed on my lips.

We kissed for a few minutes until someone cleared her throat behind us. We broke apart.

I glanced back.

Eunice waited inside the doorway, holding a plate of treats. "Meredith said to share these with the staff. Since we're the only ones here, I guess it goes to you. Warning, though, it's the healthy stuff."

"Thanks." I laughed, taking her tray and setting it down on the coffee table. "Are you working this evening?"

"Yeah, I don't really have a great home to go back to, and I like the extra money. So, I usually agree to stay on, in case the family needs me."

"You stay every year?" I asked.

"Pretty much, yeah."

Sadly, I had never noticed that before. Now that I thought about it, Eunice had always been around on Christmas Day. Knowing the old me, I probably yelled and made her holiday a living nightmare. The guilt and shame of the "jerk me" slammed into my gut hard. How could I repay this woman for years of agony?

If I returned to my old life, I would make it my goal to make everything better for her life and improve all of this down here. To start, the staff needed a better fireplace, a bigger bathroom with a tub and shower, fluffier blankets, nicer pillows, better paintings, hotter heat, and, of course, cuter outfits. "Did you want to join us?" I waved at the empty chair.

Eunice's eyes and mouth widened.

I knew, without a doubt, I had not in my former life nor in this alternative hell ever asked this woman to join me for anything. I couldn't blame her for being a little shocked.

Slowly, she lowered into the rocking chair across from us, but her expression remained guarded.

"Where's home?" I asked to smooth the thick air.

"I'm moved from France when I was little. My family stayed here until my senior year of high school. I had danced ballet my whole life, so when they decided to go back to France, I stayed and moved to New York City. Of course, I hoped to make it in the dancing world." She rocked in the chair, smiling, her eyes appeared distant as she recollected old memories. "And I almost did. I danced for about six months for a company, but then I broke the tibia bone in my ankle. The doctor said it would never fully recover. At first, I thought my life was over, but then I was offered a teaching job at a dance studio in Los Angeles. So, I moved again. But within less than a year, the studio closed down, and I had nothing again. So, in an effort to survive…" She placed her arms out in front of her, as if grabbing the world with her embrace. "This was it. My big break."

I never knew. How could I? I didn't ask. I forced her to shut up and be quiet and bring me my tea. I had never allowed this amazing woman to tell me her story. "Why have you stayed here so long? Don't you want to teach anymore?" I reached for an orange cookie, not sure what might be inside, carrots maybe, and waited for her response.

Eunice rocked, her gaze on the flickering fire. She

didn't look away as she answered. "Yes and no. Of course, I want to teach. And of course, who likes cleaning after people for a living? But I was so burnt-out and broken when I came here that I appreciated the laid-back lifestyle. I know when to get up and what I'm supposed to do. Mr. and Mrs. Tremaine seem to like me. Eventually, I might get back out there, but for now, I'm okay."

Why had I been so mean to her? I took a bite of the cookie as a distraction but spit it back onto a napkin.

Henry laughed. "No good?"

I contorted my face. "No *bueno*."

Henry reached for a cake with green specs. He sniffed it and then popped it in his mouth.

I watched his eyes to see his reaction.

He bobbed his head back and forth as he chewed. "That actually wasn't too bad."

"What was it?" Eunice asked.

"I think zucchini bread."

"Vegetables do not belong in dessert." I crossed my arms and pushed back into the cushions.

Henry lifted another square from the plate and brought it toward my nose.

I twisted my face away.

But he brought it to the other side.

I shook my head, pinning my lips tightly together. "Uh, uh. You can't make me."

He laughed, not relenting. "Just try it."

I giggled, squirming away.

"Don't be such a baby. Try it." He waved it under my nose.

As if to best me, Eunice reached for a piece and popped it in her mouth.

"See, both Eunice and I did it, and we're still alive. Your turn, woosie."

I narrowed my eyes. "You're relentless."

"True."

He held the square under my nose. It smelt of nutmeg and molasses. Maybe it wouldn't be too bad. I opened my mouth.

He set it on my tongue.

I closed my mouth and chewed.

"Well?"

Okay, it wasn't too bad. But I would not give him the satisfaction of being right. "Like I said, vegetables do not belong in dessert."

"You're lying. You liked it." He tickled my side.

I scrambled away.

"Well, I'm beat." Eunice rocked forward to her feet. "I'll see you two kids in the morning."

"Night," Henry and I said in unison.

Once alone, Henry gave me a soft, sweet kiss, then rose and helped me to my feet.

I held him for a while, comforted in his embrace.

"We should probably get to bed, too. We wouldn't want to miss Santa," he said.

I laughed. "Santa already came for me. It's you who doesn't want to miss Santa."

"Maybe Santa gives more than one gift." He winked, kissed my cheek, and walked toward his room on the other end of the hall.

I sauntered down the hall to my own place. I closed the door and shivered. The room had a slight chill. I dressed into a T-shirt and sweats, then slid in between the sheets and pulled the thin covers tight around my chin. *Yes, the staff needs much better blankets.* I finally warmed, relaxed, and almost drifted to sleep when my heart shot into my stomach. *We forgot Meredith's gift.* I flew to my feet and ran to Henry's door. I raised my fist to knock.

The door flung open.

"Meredith's gift," we said together, then both laughed.

Holding my hand, he led me down a back corridor to the garage. He opened the door and flipped on the light.

In the middle of the open space waited a bassinet with a big blue bow.

Instantly, the blood drained from my head, and stars floated in my vision. Dizzy, I grabbed the wall and blinked several times to stay upright, then lowered myself to the step.

"Do you think this is it?" he asked, staring at the bassinet. "I mean, that's an odd present for a guy."

"I don't think she's told him yet."

"Told him yet?" Henry glanced at me.

"That's she's pregnant." I wiped at my wet cheeks. "Surprise, it's the boy you always wanted, but never had. Surprise, you're now a daddy for the first time. Surprise…" My voice trailed off, as I could no longer speak.

Henry knelt in front of me and drew my hands into his.

He alone got it.

His thumb lifted a tear about to fall from my cheek. "It's only a week left, and he'll remember you."

"Yeah, but this kid will be a *good* kid. Not like me—evil and wretched enough to wish me away."

"A parent's love is unconditional. I have to believe

that. Sure, he was angry enough to wish a horrible curse on you, but I think he did that out of love, not spite."

I thought about that. "Maybe."

Henry placed his hands at my waist and guided me to my feet.

I fell into his arms. His hug, warm and calming, comforted me like nothing else. I rested there for a while, not wanting to let go. Finally, I stepped back and nodded toward the crib. "We better carry it inside and get to bed."

"Are you okay?"

"I'm trying. Come on."

He nodded, then reached for one side of the rail.

I lifted the other. Bulkier than heavy, it took a few tries to get it through the doorway and into the living room under the tree. I adjusted the tilted bow, which spurred a memory of adjusting Dad's tie. *Always crooked.* I smiled, despite how I felt.

Henry slapped his hands together. "Well, that's that."

"Yes, that's that. Night." I kissed Henry's cheek and walked back to my room.

Inside, I lay down and stared at the popcorn ceiling. A million thoughts plagued my mind. I tried to subdue them one by one, so I could fall asleep. Apparently, every day provided a decision to be happy or dwell on the negative. I spent the better time of my adolescence on the latter, but now, I was over it. For the first time, I desired to change, to be a pleasant human being, and to learn to love. I choose to find freedom. I started to believe that, in the end, it would all work out. I rolled over and drifted off in that knowledge.

Chapter Twenty-One

I rolled onto my back and opened my eyes. Christmas morning had arrived. I grinned, then swung my feet over the side of the bed and hurried to get ready before Henry saw me. We wanted the "real Christmas experience," so we promised no changing, but doing Christmas in our pj's. Of course, my pj's consisted of a T-shirt, sweats, and matching gray hoodie. What I wouldn't give for my burgundy silk pajamas and matching robe. I tiptoed down the hall to the bathroom, got presentable, and then stopped by the kitchen to commandeer muffins and two cups of coffee. Inside the staff lounge, I found Henry starting a fire in the stove. "Merry Christmas."

Henry flicked a match into the opening and grinned. "Merry Christmas!"

I set my haul on the coffee table, and then put my arms out for a hug.

He filled them and kissed me soft and slow.

"So, I have a gift for you," I said, unraveling from his hold.

He rubbed his hands together and dropped on the couch. "Hit me."

I reached under the pitiful Christmas tree Eunice had decorated earlier that week and pulled out a long red envelope. "Merry Christmas."

Henry grinned and reached for it.

I cuddled up next to his side, so excited for him to open it. The decision to do this wasn't instant. It took me a while to accept how perfect this gift would be.

He slid his finger along the crease and ripped the side open. He blew into the envelope, then withdrew the white calendar page and business card. He stared at the card. "I don't understand."

I smiled. "Read what is happening on December 30th."

He opened the month calendar page, and his eyes scrolled to the bottom. "Appointment with Mr. Tremaine, 3 p.m." Henry peered up at me with a wrinkled brow.

"Don't you get it? I got you an appointment with my dad to pitch your screenplay."

His mouth fell open. Tears pooled in his eyes. "But how? I thought…"

I licked my lips, proud of this moment. "My dad might not remember me, but I still have the inside scoop on how his system works. I have watched the process a million times and know all the back channels. I just used the inside scoop, pretending to be other people who he respects."

He sniffed. "But I thought you didn't want me to use him for my gain."

I shrugged. "You're not. I am. I made it happen. You didn't do anything other than love me. That was enough. I love you—"

The word *love* permeated the room like thick perfume.

"You love me?" He scooted so that our thighs touched and grazed his lips across mine. "And I love you, Cynthia. Thank you. It's perfect."

We kissed again.

I can't remember a time in my life when I experienced more happiness. I didn't want it to end. Nothing could take this emotion from me. I wouldn't let it.

"I need to ask you something," he said.

"Sure, what?" I asked.

His stare gazed deep into mine, searching. All merriment dissolved from his face, replaced by a grim, serious expression.

Now I worried. Maybe I had expressed happiness too soon. My smile faded, replaced by fear, now nervous my joyful balloon might be popped.

"You're returning to the old life in a week, right?"

I nodded. "It's the hope, yeah."

"What happens to me? To us?"

I hadn't let myself think about that too much. Mainly because I didn't like the answer. In truth, I already realized we would not remember each other. I would likely go back to just thinking of him as a working man, but I hoped the change in me would give him a chance. In this moment, I could not imagine a world where I did not love this guy. But this was the fantasy—the planet of my past and future. Where I planned to return did not have him in it. "I don't think you'll remember me."

His hand slid to the back of my neck, and he cupped his hand around the base of my head.

His lips found mine, and he kissed me passionately, and then his mouth moved to my ear, his breath warm.

"Then don't go."

I untangled from his arms and pushed back. "But I

have to."

Henry got to his feet and started to pace. "You don't have to. You could ask the fairy godmother to let you stay. With me."

Though I loved that he wanted me to stay and had come to believe me, I could not grant this request. It wasn't about the money. Not anymore. It was about the fact I loved my father too much. I had twenty plus years loving Dad; I had only loved Henry for a few months. "I miss my dad."

Henry walked around the coffee table and held out the red envelope. "Cindy, I need you. Don't you see that? It's all I want. I'd give up my dream, all of it, to have you in my life. Please stay with me."

His words sounded crazy, insane even. I rejected the envelope. "You could not give everything up for some girl you've only known for a few months."

He slumped down to the coffee table and sighed. "You're not just *some* girl."

I leaned forward and kissed the top of his head, then cupped my palms around his jaw and directed his face to see mine. "Henry, I love you more than I thought possible. There's a strong connection between us, and I feel that, too. But this isn't real. This isn't who I am or where I belong. It's a fairy tale. A messed-up one, but one and the same. I need to love you in my rightful place in the world. Not here. Not like this." I caressed his cheek. "You could not give up your dad for me. King is important to you, am I right?"

He nodded with defeat in his eyes.

"Like my dad is important to me. I want him back, but I promise, I will do whatever it takes to find you again."

"What if you don't remember me?"

I rubbed my hand across his closely shaved cheek and grinned. "I will never forget how you make me feel. No curse could undo that. You're my hero...my prince. If we're meant to be, fate will intervene. I have to believe that."

We wrapped our arms around each other and hugged.

"Now, let's drink our coffee before it gets cold."

He shifted back up to the couch and reached for a mug. He held it out. "Cheers. To the girl I love."

I picked up the other cup and clanked it to his. "To the girl who loves him back."

He sipped, a smile on his face, but sorrow in his eyes.

I hadn't convinced him. How could I? I wasn't convinced, either. But what could I do? The New Year would be here in a week, and my life would change for better or worse, with or without Henry. Nothing could stop that now.

Chapter Twenty-Two

Later that day, Henry opened the car door.

I had never been in East LA before, and my sense of fear tingled at high alert. I stepped out and peered up at the diminutive, one-bedroom yellow home just beyond the walkway.

A patch of dry gold earth stretched out in front, looking more like a collection of weeds than grass. Birds of paradise and various shrubs hid part of the house. All the windows were protected by rust-colored bars, and the driveway only had room for one car. Mexican music filtered from several houses in the neighborhood, along with dogs barking and babies crying. Several pairs of shoes hung from the telephone wire, and trash littered the gutters.

Henry grabbed my hand and led me forward. "Come on. It's safe."

We crossed a stone path to a metal security door and knocked.

Pat opened the door. "Oh good. You two made it. Come in, come in. Rosa is cooking up a storm in here."

I crept inside, slowly and unsure.

The house smelled of bacon and melted butter. The wooden floors contained a mauve sofa, matching love seat, a pressed-wood coffee table filled with kid's toys and books, and a small TV on a black crate.

I started to walk forward when a large chocolate

lab leapt on me. Startled, I yelped.

The dog licked my arm and pushed me into the wall.

I tried to block him with my knee out.

Eunice walked in and laughed. "I see Cindy met Bruno."

"Down, Bruno." Pat tugged on the dog's collar. "Leave the poor lady alone." He led the lab by his collar and out the back screen door.

"Are you okay?" Henry asked with an amused grin.

I narrowed my eyes. "Not that you helped or anything."

Eunice sat by a guy with black hair and matching mustache. She waved for us to join them on the sofa. "Have you met my fiancé, Jose?"

"Of course." Henry shook Jose's hand. "Jose's the one who told my friend about the job. How've you been, man?"

I recognized Jose, but I never knew who he was before. Why would I? I barely paid attention to our workers, let alone the people who knew the workers. So, Eunice did have someone who loved her.

"Good, good." He looked at me. "And Cindy, right?"

I grinned. "That's right. I work with Eunice."

He didn't smile back.

I sensed that Eunice had shared our encounters with her man. Most likely, he hated me. Not that I could really blame him. I'd be less than friendly to someone who treated Henry badly, too.

Rosa appeared in the doorway dressed in a pink apron covered in flour. "Okay, everyone. It's time to eat. I hope you brought a big appetite."

We all got up and shifted toward the tiny dining room. Rosa's husband perched in the corner, looking oddly enormous in the space. A little girl with black curls sat in a highchair next to him, and another sat on a booster chair. They were spitting images of Rosa—a little plump with kind brown eyes.

"So, we probably won't all fit at the table, but fill your plates and then eat wherever you like." She pointed to pans around the stove and covering the counters. "I'll get out of the way, so you can walk through."

Henry reached for two plates and handed me one.

The white dish was hard like glass but wasn't glass. *Interesting.* We each passed the various pans. I chose scrambled eggs covered in cheddar, lots of bacon, cinnamon rolls, hash browns smothered in cheese, and some fresh strawberries. Each bite reminded me of why Dad hired her. *Rosa could cook.*

I didn't talk much, but I listened. They told story after story about some of the most amazing adventures. These people had little when it came to wealth; yet, they had so much when it came to life. I began to realize, pleasure existed beyond stuff. Friendship harbored the gratification I craved. It was not material things. All the drinking and villainy stemmed from my desire to forget the past, but I now recognized happiness held the key to healing. Not forgetting or pushing it down, which only kept the pain hidden, not released.

I cracked a piece of bacon and dropped it in my mouth, trying not to cry. This was not the time or place to have a pity party. *Keep it together, girl.*

"Cindy, how are you?" Eunice asked.

She had picked the worst time possible to talk to me. I panicked. My voice would crack if I tried to talk right now. I offered a closed-mouth smile and a shrug.

Henry squeezed my knee.

I rested my head on his shoulder for a moment.

"Well, I'm glad you came," Rosa said simply.

That had to take a swallow of pride for her to say. I figured that was Rosa speak for *I forgive you.* "Me, too. Thanks."

Her little girl ran to my side and dropped a cloth doll in my lap.

I grinned and then glanced at Rosa. "How old is your daughter?"

"Perla is three."

"Nice to meet you, Perla. I like your doll," I said in a high-pitched tone only meant for little kids.

"Santa brought it." She beamed.

"Oh, well, Santa's pretty incredible, huh?"

She nodded with a big smile. "What did Santa bring you?"

"Shoe glue." I laughed.

Perla wrinkled her nose. "You might want to be a better girl next year."

For a second, no one breathed.

I giggled, then the whole room erupted in a laughter. Never a truer statement had been uttered. "Awe, the wisdom of children," I said. "I think you're right, Perla. I think you're right."

****

Once we all returned from Rosa's house, Eunice and I were asked to help with the cleanup of the living room.

Dad sat on the couch, rubbing Meredith's belly.

The two sisters played with new technology in their hands.

I swallowed my emotions and shoved discarded paper and bows into the garbage bag.

Gabby noticed me and tapped my shoulder. "Hey, Cindy, we got you something."

I raised an eyebrow. "Really? Me?"

"Really. You." Gabby and Charlotte exchanged glances and smiled.

Gabby moved to the fireplace and lifted a five-by-eight wrapped package and handed it out.

I held it, surprised by their generosity.

"Open it, silly," Charlotte said.

I nodded through the tears in my eyes and unwrapped it. Instantly, I understood. It was a dream planner.

"Now, you can dream," Gabby said. "And when you're ready, we're here to help you achieve it."

I hugged both of them. How I had misjudged these two girls? I couldn't wait to return to my old life and to be nicer to both of them. I wanted to become their friend. They were truly remarkable. "Thank you. It means a lot."

"Great." Gabby and Charlotte returned to what they were doing before.

I carried the trash out into the back of the house and tossed it in the dumpster. I turned to go back in.

Henry came behind me and covered my eyes. "Guess who?"

"Um, the gardener," I joked.

"Try again."

"The cute limo driver?" I said, half-laughing but half scared. "What are you doing?"

"I promised you another present."

"Better than shoe glue? I'm not sure you can top that."

He led me forward about ten feet and removed his hands. "Are you sure about that?"

A patch of snow covered a small portion of the backyard. "No way. Snow in Southern California? How'd you do it?"

"For you, dear, anything." He handed me some gloves and then slipped a hand in the small of my back and drew me closer to my gift. Once at the edge, he bent down and formed a snowball.

I hurried to make one of my own, but before I could, ice shattered apart on my arm. "Oh, you!" I yelled playfully, then rolled one myself and pitched it. It flew by his left ear. I leaned again and tried to make another one. But before I could pitch it, I felt a ball hit my hunched back. "You're so going to get it!" I tossed and nailed my intended target this time.

We scampered around scooping, throwing, ducking, and laughing. Never could I remember a better time than that moment. One smacked me in the cheek. It stung a bit, but I didn't care. I just retaliated.

He ducked but not fast enough. It caught him in the shoulder. Henry warmed up to make another one.

But I charged him and knocked him back to the earth and pinned him down. "Got you."

"Do you now?" He laughed, then started to tickle my side.

"Stop that. I'm extremely ticklish." I squirmed away.

But he followed. "I gathered that, which of course just makes me want to do it more." Henry twisted his finger next to my rib cage.

I jumped to my feet and backed away. "Okay, mister. Now you've done it."

Henry winked, a subtle challenge.

I rolled a big snowball and pretended to throw.

He ducked, but his face came back up.

I tossed it for real. It landed hard against his chin. I flung my arms in the air. "Yes! And she scores."

Henry wiped the ice from his face, smiling. "Come here, you." He wagged his pointer finger back and forth, beckoning me toward him.

I shook my head.

He nodded and stepped toward me.

I paced back, afraid of what he might do.

He countered. "I promise I won't tickle you." He walked another step closer.

"Promise?" I challenged, remaining put this time.

"Have I ever lied to you before?"

I smiled. "Not that I know of."

His stride being longer than mine brought him to me. He yanked off his glove and caressed my cheek with cool hands. His tone and expression melted and turned more serious. "Merry Christmas, Cindy."

"Merry Christmas, Henry."

His lips swept mine. "You know, I love you?"

I kissed him again, only longer and more fervently, then pulled back, with fresh tears in my eyes. "And I love you, too. My prince. My hero. Thank you for rescuing me from myself. I could not have done this without you."

"I don't want you to go."

"I know. I wish I could have both." I touched my gloved hand to his chin. "But imagine a world without your father. When he's all you've had for so long."

"I desperately hope this is just some fantasy you made up and not reality."

"Then we'd be a fantasy, too." I shifted back and sighed. "I need this to be real. You, me, all of it. For once, I feel happy. Despite all that has happened, I now understand love. I wouldn't give this experience up for anything. But—" I shuffled forward. My shoes crunching in the melting ice. "I have to get back, even if that hurts, too."

"I know." His arm wrapped around my shoulders, and he pulled me in for a hug.

We held each other for a long while.

Though I knew that our time together would end soon, I was happy it hadn't ended yet.

Chapter Twenty-Three

In the hallway mirror, I caught my reflection. I set the tray of sushi on a small table and stared at the black maid uniform in the glass. Meredith had rented us special uniforms for the party. This was better than the gray one, but I prayed this was the last time I'd ever have to wear one.

Henry slid his arms around my waist and leaned to peer over my shoulder. "Even in a uniform, you're still the hottest girl in the room."

I laughed and spun around to kiss him.

He wore a red tuxedo, complete with tails, a black bow tie, matching pants, and a white shirt.

Dad wanted him to resemble a footman for the night. I adjusted his tie and smiled. "You don't look so bad yourself. I kind of like this look on you."

"So, I have good news?" Henry said.

"I love good news. What is it?"

"Your dad is interested in my script."

I squealed, then covered my mouth and glanced around to make sure no one heard me. "That's wonderful, Henry. I'm so happy for you."

He kissed me. "Thank you."

"Of course."

Across the room, Meredith clanked a glass. "Okay, everyone. It's almost time. Grab a glass, if you haven't got one already." She waved everyone to a table filled with champagne flutes.

Guests retrieved one and stepped back to watch the big screen TV on the wall.

Henry gazed into my eyes.

Tears welled in mine. This was it; the last time he would hold me. I didn't know what I wanted more. Part of me desired to stay with him forever and forget the rest, but I peered over at my dad, now standing with an arm around Meredith. The man who raised me, who loved me through everything, I could not live without him knowing who I was. The hope would be, I could pursue Henry again. I prayed the new me would give him a chance. I traced his jaw with my finger and then swept my lips across his. "I have to go."

"I don't want you to." Henry held my waist tighter.

I kissed him again. "Me, either."

"Then don't."

"You know I have to." I pulled him closer and whispered in his ear, "But I'll find you. I promise."

"Ten…nine…" Everyone started the countdown as the New York apple descended on the big screen. "Eight…seven…"

"I'm sorry." I broke free from his arms, rushed out the front door, and sprinted down the steps. One of my torn shoes flew off somewhere, but I could not stop to retrieve it. I needed to reach the limo before the stroke of midnight. Once my foot hit the last step, I ran across the driveway and thrust open the limo door, just as fireworks blasted in the sky.

My fairy godmother sat regally, clearly waiting for my arrival. Her makeup and hair were flawless, as always.

I slid across the empty seat, afraid to close the

door, but it slammed on its own anyway. The locks snapped in place, and I stared at the woman who had brought me so much pain and an incredible amount of joy. Loss and love—I wanted to hug her and punch her. My pulse drummed in my ears; my breath stuck in my throat as I grappled to breathe. How would this end? Did I do enough? Or would she punish me forever?

"I see you made it on time."

Her tone sounded softer and kinder than I remembered from before. "I did." I managed a slight grin, despite the factory of emotions rising inside me.

"Would you say that you are now a decent human being, Cynthia?"

"I believe so. Or at least, I hope to keep working on becoming one."

The woman rested her tongue on her top lip and inclined forward.

Her expression was vacant of any real tell. Would she change me back? Did I prove myself? Who knew? I sucked in a deep breath of air, hoping to stop my pulse from galloping in my neck.

"You wonder if you did enough. If you are worthy of returning to your old life?" she asked.

I nodded, unable to speak. My vision blurred. My cheeks burned from hot tears.

"Tell me, young lady, do *you* think you did enough? Are you worthy to be changed back?"

I shrugged, still unable to find my voice.

"You don't know?" One of her perfectly shaped eyebrows lifted. She puckered her lips and glared.

"I don't know, what's worthy?" I wheezed through the turbulent feelings. "I only know that I love my dad, and I love Henry. Either way, I win. Either way, I lose.

But I know I am different, and I have to accept what happens. But ultimately, I want to go back, not for money or stuff, but just for my dad. I need to make things right with him. In truth, I'd stay in this life, if it meant I could have my father, too."

Her mouth faded from contempt to a smile. "I've been watching you, Cindy, and I have to say, I am quite impressed. I honestly think you are the worst case I have ever had to deal with in over 200 years."

"Thanks," I said dryly.

She folded her hands and scooted forward. "But I also think you are my biggest success."

"Really?" I couldn't believe it. Her words warmed my heart.

"Really." She snapped her fingers.

My clothes squeezed my torso. I glanced down to see the maid's uniform had transformed into the blue dress from the birthday party. The ripped shoes were now replaced with my glass-rhinestone pumps. Emotion overwhelmed my chest, and I burst into sobs. "Thank you, thank you so much."

She reached across and touched my hand. "Be good, Cindy."

"I will. I promise."

"I believe you." She grinned. "Are you going to be okay?"

"I'm going to miss my best friend, Henry." A sob choked my throat. "I know I couldn't have made it without him. Though I'm happy to return to my dad, I'm going to miss Henry terribly."

"I understand." She patted my knee and grinned. "But who knows, things have a way of working themselves out."

"It's crazy to say this, but thank you. I got to feel true love, if only for a moment, and that made it all worth it."

"You're very welcome." She winked, snapped, and then vanished.

I blinked to be sure. Yes, she was gone. I tugged on the door handle, and it surprisingly opened without a hitch. From inside the mansion came sounds of merriment as people cheered. A new year had started, and I had no idea what it would hold. I shut the limo door and inched toward the stairs, afraid to go inside. I felt alone, lost, and unsure of what would come next.

Something scraped to my left. I stopped and looked. In the dimly lit driveway, I made out Henry's silhouette walking toward me.

"I think you dropped this." He handed out the torn canvas shoe lost on the stairs.

I didn't reach for it. Hot tears slid down my cheeks.

"It's not yours?" He peered down at the ratty cloth slipper in his hand. "Because I'm in love with the woman who fits this shoe."

"You remember me?" My pulse quickened. I dabbed at my eyes with the back of my hand.

A smile crept across his face. "What, the spoiled rich girl who likes to tell me off every chance she gets?" He reached out a thumb and wiped a tear away. "Or the crazy maid I fell in love with in the last few months?" He tossed the shoe over his shoulder and drew me in his arms.

"I don't understand." I choked with emotion as he kissed me. "How do you remember?"

"The fairy godmother paid me a visit last night and asked me if I wanted to remember you. I told her I did.

She said she'd consider it after talking with you. I didn't say anything because I didn't want to get your hopes up." He kissed the tip of my nose and offered me a closed-mouth grin. "Just now, she came again. With a snap of her fingers, I remembered both sides of the story."

I brought my lips to his and kissed him passionately. Salty and wet, but the kiss was the best I'd ever had.

"Cindy?"

I heard Dad say behind me. I jumped back and grinned, my heart racing and my eyes pooling with tears. "Dad?"

"Yeah, hon. We're getting ready to share our resolutions. Are you coming?"

I bolted toward him and wrapped my arms around him tight.

He laughed and hugged me back. "Wow, that's some hug."

"I love you so much, Dad. I'm so sorry I have been such a brat since Mom died. Will you ever forgive me?"

"Oh, honey. Of course. You know, I love you." He untangled from my arms and glanced at Henry. "Now, you and your boyfriend come in, okay. I don't want to start without you."

"Okay, Dad. We'll be right in." I crossed back to Henry and folded him into a hug.

"Are you okay?" he asked.

I rested my head on his shoulder and smiled. "Never better."

Epilogue
Almost Two Years Later

The sun beamed through my window, announcing my big day had finally come. I rolled over and grinned. I rang the bell by my bed and leapt from the mattress to the carpeted floor.

The door cracked open, and Eunice stepped inside. "You rang?"

"Good morning, my friend," I said. "Are you ready?"

"The real question is, are you?" She handed me a mug of coffee.

"Oh, you're the best." I sipped from the brim and let the warm of liquid caffeine fill my soul. "Did your dress make it back from the seamstress?"

"Yes, and it's gorgeous. I can't wait to wear it."

I patted the mattress and had her join me. "I'm glad you agreed to do this for me. You know I don't have a lot of friends."

"But you have me and—"

And as if on cue, Gabby and Charlotte rushed into the room and pounced on my bed.

Laughing, I tried not to spill my drink and slid it onto my end table.

Gabby grabbed me in a hug.

Charlotte came around her.

Eunice slid down and almost landed on the floor

but caught herself in time.

"Do you know what today is?" Gabby squealed.

"No idea." I laughed. "Please enlighten me."

"Only the most important day of your life, silly. Come on, let's get you pampered and pretty." Gabby jumped to the floor and tugged on my arm.

Charlotte mirrored the action and yanked on my other arm.

I laughed and let them drag me to a Victorian cream chair that had been placed in front of a full-length mirror the night before.

Eunice ran out of the room and returned with the makeup and hair people.

The stylist curled my long blonde hair into ringlets. She sprayed in small daisies periodically by the curls.

The makeup artist took over next, adorning my face in soft burgundy hues and dewberry lipstick. I don't know if I ever looked prettier. Well, I hoped that to be true.

Eunice and Gabby helped me slide into the princess-cut white dress with satin and beads at the top and tulle and diamonds on the bottom.

In my mind's eye, I saw Mom standing in my reflection. I resembled her in every way. I wished so much that she could be here, looking over my shoulder and telling me how beautiful I looked. I tilted my hips side to side, listening to the swish, and smiled. I fingered the necklace she gave me, resting at the base of my neck. Most people don't wear black on their wedding days, but this was important. I was sure my aunt will say otherwise, but too bad.

The sisters and Eunice left for a little while, then returned clothed in plum, tee-length dresses. The deep purple ended up being a great color for the two redheads. The three of them could not stop giggling.

I found myself following suit.

The door opened, and Meredith entered dressed in a flowy violet dress. She carried in her arms a bouquet of purple and white Gerber daisies. "You look so beautiful," she said, with tears in her eyes.

I smiled, trying to hold back my own tears.

Meredith and I had finally become great friends. I saw her more of a big sister than a mother, but I cared about her deeply.

She placed the flowers on my bed and then pulled me into a hug.

"I'm glad you're here," I said.

She dabbed her eyes. "Me, too. Now, don't go messing up our makeup."

"Yes, good idea." I sniffed and dabbed at the corner of my lids.

A photographer entered and snapped various shots around the room: several of me in the mirror, one with Meredith putting on my garter, and one with me and my sisters acting silly, sticking out our tongues. Of course, there were a bunch of serious ones, too, with us posing with flowers.

My baby brother, Luke, ran in full throttle straight at me. "Indy!"

Charlotte scooped him up before he reached me and swung him around in the air. "You can't go jumping on Cindy's dress with your shoes. She has to be pretty."

I squatted down and put my arms out. "It's okay. Come here, my boy."

Charlotte let him down, and he tottered forward with chubby arms extended.

I grinned and embraced him in a bear hug.

He kissed my cheek, then leaned his up for our usual butterfly kiss.

I obliged with the fluttering of my eyelashes to his face.

He giggled and squirmed away.

The wedding coordinator entered. "It's time."

My heart leapt almost through my chest. I couldn't believe I would soon be married to Henry—my soul mate, my hero, my prince. I patted Luke's head and stood ready for my dream to come true.

"We'll see you down there." Meredith made a kissy sound at my cheek, then scooped Luke into her arms and left.

Charlotte and Gabby each blew me a kiss, and then rushed Eunice out the door.

Dad appeared in the doorway in a black tux.

His bowtie was, of course, crooked. I stepped forward to fix it. Any hope of salvaging my makeup about went out the window. We hugged and cried.

"I'm just so proud of you," he said.

"Thanks, Dad." I sniveled. How long I had ached to hear those words? For as long as I could remember. Over the last year, I had done plenty to secure his pride. Thanks to Charlotte and Gabby, I started my own party planning company. Also, I had stopped being a brat, making friends with the staff and helping in the community. But most of all, I had aspired to be a kind person like my mother. It didn't happen overnight. It took time for people to trust me. Other than Henry, no one remembered the *maid me*. They only knew the spoiled, rude me. Every day, I walked into the kitchen and sat at the counter with Rosa. I helped her peel potatoes, snapped peas, made coffee, and cleaned dishes.

I confided in Eunice and helped her plan her own wedding. I insisted on paying for it and having it in our backyard. She soon became my best friend.

Charlotte and Gabby were now my sisters in every way. We did something together almost daily for two years.

I apologized to them for my actions. Surprisingly, they accepted.

They said they could have easily become like me had they chosen differently. They promised to help me choose joy.

I love those two like birth-siblings and could not be more grateful for who they are—quirkiness and all.

"You okay?" Dad asked.

His question broke me out of my reverie. "Yeah, just reflecting on the past two years." I folded my hand under his arm and strode with him down the stairs to the backyard. I couldn't see him yet, but I knew my future husband waited under a white, handcrafted archway covered in ivy and flowers.

Dad and I rounded the corner.

"If you all could stand for the entrance of the bride." The preacher's voice cut through the open air.

The sounds of chairs shifted on the wooden floor placed in our yard, just as the wedding march started to play.

I had butterflies in my stomach. We walked to the edge of the aisle, and there he waited—my prince charming. The man who saved me from a life without love and forgiveness. He was handsome in a white tux with a black lapel. His smile gleamed in the sun against his dark skin.

White and purple petals lined the path. Each chair on the end held a satin bow and Gerbera daisies, my favorite flower. I stepped forward down the white runner, and the audience "oohed" and "aahed," smiling and snapping pictures. But I only had eyes for the man at the end.

His eyes glistened, and his grin could not grow any wider.

"Who gives this woman in matrimony to this man?" the preacher asked.

"I do," Dad said, then kissed my cheek and joined Meredith.

I glided my palms into Henry's waiting hands.

You looked beautiful, he mouthed.

"You, too," I whispered and winked.

The preacher led us through vows and rings. Finally, I heard the words I'd waited to hear. "I now pronounce you husband and wife. You may kiss your bride."

And he did.

A word about the author...

Dr. Kimberlee Mendoza is the Dean of the School of Languages and Literature/Associate Professor of English at Wayland Baptist University where she teaches writing. When she is not working in education, she moonlights as an inspirational speaker, a graphic designer for the Wild Rose Press, a novelist of more than a dozen books, a playwright for sixteen plays, and the author a few non-fiction books, including Teaching Squirrels: How to Engage Generation Z and Create Lasting Engagement. She is also a US Army veteran. It is her biggest mission in life to help people discover their passion and then walk with them.

Other Titles by this Author
Confessions of a Con Man
Fried, Scrambled & Unequally Yoked
Love thy Sister; Guard thy Man
Oh Brother, You're Not My Keeper
Seek Ye First My Heart
The After-School Question
The Hidden Two
The Forgotten Ones
The Lost Few
Trick to Treat
Wish Upon a Rock Star

Thank you for purchasing
this publication of The Wild Rose Press, Inc.

For questions or more information
contact us at
info@thewildrosepress.com.

The Wild Rose Press, Inc.
www.thewildrosepress.com

www.ingramcontent.com/pod-product-compliance
Lightning Source LLC
Chambersburg PA
CBHW05164526062
47170CB00004B/1347